Donald MacKenzie and The Murder Room

›› This title is part of The Murder Room, our series dedicated to making available out-of-print or hard-to-find titles by classic crime writers.

Crime fiction has always held up a mirror to society. The Victorians were fascinated by sensational murder and the emerging science of detection; now we are obsessed with the forensic detail of violent death. And no other genre has so captivated and enthralled readers.

Vast troves of classic crime writing have for a long time been unavailable to all but the most dedicated frequenters of second-hand bookshops. The advent of digital publishing means that we are now able to bring you the backlists of a huge range of titles by classic and contemporary crime writers, some of which have been out of print for decades.

From the genteel amateur private eyes of the Golden Age and the femmes fatales of pulp fiction, to the morally ambiguous hard-boiled detectives of mid twentieth-century America and their descendants who walk our twenty-first century streets, The Murder Room has it all. ››

The Murder Room
Where Criminal Minds Meet

themurderroom.com

Donald MacKenzie 1908–1994

Donald MacKenzie was born in Ontario, Canada, and educated in England, Canada and Switzerland. For twenty-five years MacKenzie lived by crime in many countries. 'I went to jail,' he wrote, 'if not with depressing regularity, too often for my liking.' His last sentences were five years in the United States and three years in England, running consecutively. He began writing and selling stories when in American jail. 'I try to do exactly as I like as often as possible and I don't think I'm either psychopathic, a wayward boy, a problem of our time, a charming rogue. Or ever was.'

He had a wife, Estrela, and a daughter, and they divided their time between England, Portugal, Spain and Austria.

By Donald MacKenzie

Henry Chalice
Salute from a Dead Man (1966)
Death is a Friend (1967)
Sleep is for the Rich (1971)

John Raven
Zaleski's Percentage (1974)
Raven in Flight (1976)
Raven and the Ratcatcher
  (1976)
Raven and the Kamikaze (1977)
Raven After Dark (1979)
Raven Settles a Score (1979)
Raven and the Paperhangers
  (1980)
Raven's Revenge (1982)
Raven's Longest Night (1983)
Raven's Shadow (1984)
Nobody Here By That Name
  (1986)
A Savage State of Grace (1988)
By Any Illegal Means (1989)
Loose Cannon (1994)
The Eyes of the Goat (1992)
The Sixth Deadly Sin (1993)

Standalone novels
Nowhere to Go (1956)
The Juryman (1957)
The Scent of Danger (1958)
Dangerous Silence (1960)
Knife Edge (1961)
The Genial Stranger (1962)
Double Exposure (1963)
The Lonely Side of the River
  (1964)
Cool Sleeps Balaban (1964)
Dead Straight (1968)
Three Minus Two (1968)
Night Boat from Puerto
  Vedra (1970)
The Kyle Contract (1971)
Postscript to a Dead Letter
  (1973)
The Spreewald Collection
  (1975)
Deep, Dark and Dead (1978)
The Last of the Boatriders
  (1981)

Double Exposure

Donald MacKenzie

An Orion book

Copyright © The Estate of Donald MacKenzie 1963

The right of Donald MacKenzie to be identified as the author of this work has been asserted in accordance with the Copyright, Designs and Patents Act 1988.

This edition published by
The Orion Publishing Group Ltd
Orion House
5 Upper St Martin's Lane
London WC2H 9EA

An Hachette UK company
A CIP catalogue record for this book is available from the British Library

ISBN 978 1 4719 0571 1

www.orionbooks.co.uk

For Bob and Jeanette McCreery with the reminder that it was wet that winter.

I

THE VERDICT hushed the court to a nervous silence. Hendry was still on his feet, staring across at the jury bench incredulously. Most of the eyes there were carefully averted. Only the foreman was less fastidious. He sat with his arms folded across his chest, the jut of his chin defiant as he glared at the prisoner in the dock.

The huddle of wig and gown, high on the dais, produced an old, weary voice.

'You have been found guilty on two counts, Hendry. In the first place of being a habitual criminal with the statutory number of previous felony convictions. Is there anything you wish to say before I pass sentence on you?'

The hint of irony made Hendry's heart grow smaller. He hung on tightly to the wooden ledge, blocking the shouted abuse that clamoured in his head. He aimed the accusation squarely at the group of detectives sitting under the judge's bench.

'Go ahead and tell him, Pell – tell him who helped you frame me!'

Someone in the public gallery smothered a laugh. The three detectives at the solicitors' table changed legs self-consciously, trying not to look at Detective-Inspector Pell. He rearranged the exhibits in front of him, shaking his head.

The judge ignored the outburst. He joined thin veined hands in the pursuit of justice.

'Very well. I'll take evidence of the prisoner's antecedents.'

A warder plucked Hendry's jacket from behind. He sat down heavily, wiping his wet palms on his handkerchief. He watched Pell's confident progress from the solicitors' table to the witness stand. The detective-inspector took the oath reverently. He stood, spread-legged, lifting his bent brooding face in a pose Hendry knew full well. It was that of the honest cop – fearless but just – with a fanatical repugnance for all forms of lawbreaking. None in the courtroom would accept the suggestion that this man could use perjured testimony or planted evidence.

Pell's microphone manner had the right mixture of ease and candour. He propped his notebook on the edge of the stand and made himself heard in a rumbling voice with a North Country accent.

'Henry Pell, my lord, detective-inspector attached to New Scotland Yard. The accused's full name is Christopher Barr Hendry. He was born in Toronto, Canada, on the eleventh of August, nineteen hundred and eighteen. He was educated privately in that country and Germany. In nineteen hundred and thirty-nine, he joined the Toronto Scottish Regiment and was posted to England early the following year. He was commissioned in nineteen forty-one and seconded to the British Army for special duty.'

Here Pell held his notebook to the light, apologized to the judge for his frailty and donned spectacles.

'I'm afraid I haven't been able to get much information about Hendry's war record, sir. The authorities concerned are unwilling to co-operate. But I understand that he saw active service as a specialist on the Continent and in North Africa. He was honourably discharged in nineteen forty-five with the rank of major. That was in Canada. Six months later he returned to England. He was first convicted in this court before Justice Nelson, sir, in October nineteen forty-eight. He was sentenced to two years' imprisonment for stealing jewellery and released in nineteen fifty. In June nineteen fifty-three he was convicted at Hampshire Assizes on a charge of safe-breaking. He served three years and was released in July nineteen fifty-five. His last conviction was in January nineteen fifty-seven when he was sentenced to five years' imprisonment at the County of London Sessions. A large sum in securities was involved on this occasion, my lord. None of it was recovered. Hendry last left jail in November nineteen sixty. Three weeks ago, in the Solicitors' Room at Brixton Prison, I served notice on the defendant that he would be proceeded against as a habitual criminal under the terms of the Criminal Justice Act, nineteen forty-eight. Your Lordship has a copy of the prison commissioners' report in this matter. It states that in their opinion Hendry is unsuitable for corrective training but fit for preventive detention. Thank you, sir.' He snapped the elastic on his notebook, the sound like a shot over the public address system. His belly was in and his shoulders back. It was the stance of a man doing a distasteful duty. The judge transferred his weight from one buttock to another. He closed his eyes, massaging the angry red line across the bridge of his nose. When he had put away his spectacles he took a hard look at the prisoner. His mouth screwed into open disapproval. He leaned towards Pell in the witness box, one just man to another. The record would leave no doubt of his impartiality.

'This is a case, Inspector, where it is essential to admit the fullest evidence of character. The defendant has seen fit to call no witnesses on his behalf. It is therefore doubly the duty of the court to hear whatever is known in the prisoner's favour as well as that which weighs against him. As a police officer of considerable experience you will be aware of this?'

Pell's consciousness of his responsibility was manifest. 'Yes, my lord.'

The judge nodded away to himself. 'Exactly. But if my understanding is correct, you are telling the court that – other than in the Army – this man has done no honest work in his life?'

Pell hesitated. At the end his answer was rueful. 'It isn't easy to give a fair reply, my lord. The prisoner has always refused to answer questions about his home life and so on. Certainly we have no record of him being employed. There is one other thing, sir – I am instructed by my superiors at New Scotland Yard to say that they regard this man as a dangerous and determined criminal.'

The judge's hands made a tent over which he considered counsels' bench. 'Have you any questions for the police officer, Mr Cameron?' He gave the impression that he found the suggestion in bad taste.

Hendry's lawyer came to his feet, holding a couple of pieces of paper. His pale face was puzzled.

'There's one thing I'm not quite clear about, Inspector. Do you expect everyone you arrest to provide you with a sort of detailed autobiography? Doesn't it occur to you that there are men who might be reluctant to involve friends and family in a police investigation?'

Pell shook his head doggedly. 'There's nothing in a police investigation for an innocent man to be afraid of, Mr Cameron.'

Cameron smiled bleakly. 'That must be a matter of opinion. We are all obliged to the learned judge for his instructions on the need for fairness. Let me remind you of your description of the prisoner – "a dangerous and determined criminal". Would you call that a fair statement, Inspector?'

Pell was patient. 'I didn't say it was fair or unfair. I'm doing the same as any other police officer, sir – obeying orders.'

The lawyer's tone was sarcastic. 'I'm certain we all appreciate your dilemma, Inspector. It's just possible that my source of information is not available to Scotland Yard. You must correct me if you disagree with anything I say. Christopher Hendry is the only son of highly respectable parents who were divorced shortly after his birth. I have in my hand two letters. The first is from a Toronto clergyman. Mrs Hendry lived in this gentleman's parish. He tells me that Hendry was the sole support of his mother until her death four years ago. The other letter is from the Canadian Consulate in Marrakesh, Morocco. I quote: ". . . in answer to your inquiry, the *Foncière Marocaine* was an import-export company registered here in nineteen forty-six. The President on record was Christopher Barr Hendry. This company ceased to operate in nineteen forty-eight, paying its creditors a hundred cents on the dollar." Is there anything there that you'd like to dispute, Inspector?'

Pell's concession was unexpected. 'Nothing at all, sir.'

Cameron looked eloquently at the judge. 'No more questions, my lord!' He whipped the gown under him and sat down.

Hendry watched Pell stride back to the table. The detective

4

started packing the exhibits into a canvas bag. He lingered over each article, the skeleton keys and files, the plan and pictures of the burgled house ripped from a copy of *Country Life*. Last of all came a plaster cast of a footprint. Hendry had never seen any of these things in his life. All except the footcast had been found in his cottage, taped to a cistern in the lavatory.

Cameron's late stand was useless. With a verdict of guilty already going for him Pell had no reason to worry. The judge bent over the front of his dais, whispering to his clerk. He straightened his back to smile across the court.

'You have discharged your duty very properly, members of the jury. I have given instructions for your names to be removed from the register for five years. You will no doubt be glad to hear that what I have to say next is only of secondary interest to you.'

The foreman blew his nose. He had listened to Hendry's record with obvious satisfaction. A woman in the row behind him said something in his ear. He climbed up, redfaced, with mumbled thanks.

The judge addressed himself to the glass dome in the ceiling.

'I intend to put this case back until tomorrow morning at ten-thirty for sentencing. If counsel for the defence has anything to say in mitigation at that time, I shall of course hear him.'

He bobbed his head, first left, then right, and disappeared through a door in the panelling behind him.

There was a sudden confusion of shuffling feet and belated throat-clearing. Pell sat with folded arms looking up at the dock. He smiled as his glance met Hendry's.

'Come on, mate, let's have you.'

The voice in the Canadian's ear was without malice. He turned under the warder's guidance to face the public gallery. The front row bulged as the spectators battled for a better view of the prisoner. He raised his head impassively. This was society. Curious, afraid, condemning. The staring eyes were still hungry – dissatisfied at having missed the sentencing.

Some would be back in the morning. He focused on a woman who had all the glamour of a parsnip and screwed his features into the mask of malevolence she expected. He watched her flinch, grinned, then followed the warder down the steps.

The heavy door banged on the narrow box of steel, tile and concrete. The choice of manœuvre now was uncomplicated. He either walked the three paces from one end of the cell to the other or sat down. He pushed the bundle of dirty shirts along the bench, making room.

For five days the scales upstairs had been tipping under the weight of speech, testimony and exhibit. Now they sagged under the final burden of his criminal record. All that remained was for the judge to make the tally.

He searched his pockets for a match – split its red head with a pin. Where he was going, such things mattered. Half-a-match or a cigarette butt could place a man in a superior position. Someone banged a key in the lock outside, spun it with practised flamboyancy. The door opened on the jailer who had stood in the dock with him. A big, creaking man with a guileless face. Without his uniform cap he looked years older. He put his fingers to his nose with elaborate disgust.

'Blimey, what are you smoking – old socks?' He threw a package of cigarettes into the cell without change of expression. 'Show a leg – your mouthpiece wants to see you.'

Hendry put the cigarettes in his pocket. Jailhouse philosophy held the only good screw to be a dead one. It made no more sense than the rest of the thief's creed – the indomitable virtue of the woman left outside, the blind loyalty of a rap partner. The whole was an image that flattered but one in which you didn't necessarily believe.

He got up, smiling. Protocol must be observed, the pedestrian humour answered in kind.

'You're a good man, Joe. I'll recommend you for parole.'

The Solicitors' Room was brilliant after the twilight of the cell. He took a seat across the table from Cameron. His lawyer was still gowned, the actor's mobile face composed to concern.

'You can't say I didn't warn you, Hendry. You know what

I've thought from the beginning. If you'd let me call Mrs Jeffries we'd have stood a chance. I don't care about the prosecution proving association. An alibi given by a woman still carries weight. I'm going by the book.'

'Don't,' said Hendry shortly. 'It doesn't always work. According to the book, a dirty frameup like this wouldn't have gotten by a magistrates' court. If this judge ever heard of it, he keeps a secret well. Nobody wants to hear evidence where I was that night, Cameron. They *know*. What's more they can prove it. Don't get the idea I'm a hero – it's just that calling Mrs Jeffries would have been useless. The jury would have believed her as much as they did me. There's something else – what do you think the reporters would have done to her?'

Cameron's upper lip twitched. 'Chivalry. Ah well – we'll have to have a go on appeal. Parts of that summing-up were vicious.' The thought seemed to give him comfort.

Hendry shook his head. 'He'll run rings round you. What's the trial record going to show – words! None of that old goat's pantomiming – none of the stuff that counted with the jury. Looking sick when I gave evidence – smirking when Pell and the others took the stand. You'll see none of that. You can't *put* it on paper, for Cris-sakes. He didn't set a foot wrong – there's nothing that's reversible. I know when I'm beaten, Cameron. There isn't going to be an appeal.'

Cameron slid his wig higher on his forehead. 'It's entirely up to you, of course. Anyway I'll be in court tomorrow morning. You can think about it overnight. We'll have to do the best we can with your army record.'

Hendry ran his fingers slowly along the polished edge of the table.

'How about you, Cameron. Do you think I'm guilty?'

The lawyer's mouth was nervous. 'I'll tell you what I think – you're your own worst enemy. I talked to someone at the Yard about you three days ago. One way and another you seem to have been a bigger headache to them than twenty old lags who play according to the rules. You must have gone out of your way to antagonize the police over the past few years.

Somebody comes to see you on a routine inquiry – when you've got a record like yours, why not? But to put the interview on tape – offer it to the BBC as an example of police procedure. This is childish, Hendry. For the rest, I'm bound to believe in your innocence.'

'Sure,' Hendry said quietly. Deep down Cameron knew the futility of an appeal as well as he did. It was the last hopeless defiance designed to make years of skilly more palatable. In any case, what little money was left Bernadette needed. The jury's verdict would come as a shock to her. She had the American's belief in the special sanctity of British justice. Maybe this time she'd get the message – when the law was determined it was time for you to go, you went. It wouldn't be the last illusion she would have to shed. There was the logic of a clean and irrevocable break between them to face. And if love had nothing to do with logic, it had nothing to do with a prison cell either.

He wrapped one hand round the other. His fist was as unsteady as his voice. The last truth had to be dragged to light.

'You're going to walk out of here back to all the familiar things that mean home, Cameron. I've lost all that – been robbed of it. I've got to know who's behind Pell – who helped him frame me? You must have an idea – you guys talk to one another when you take off those wigs.'

The lawyer looked at him in silence before turning his head away. 'I don't know. And if I did, I still wouldn't tell you.'

2

THICK RED curtains insulated the room from the chilly Knightsbridge square. The walls were bare of all distracting ornament. A single engraving hung over the fluted fireplace – perpetuating the bellicosity of some minor Crimean general. A leather-topped desk separated the two seated men. The glowing stove wafted hot air impartially – the room smelled faintly of vaporized oil.

Gaunt controlled his impatience. For eleven years he'd been in and out of this room, each summons a challenge to duty and ingenuity. The elements were unvarying. Danger, difficulty, and urgency. Had any factor been missing, the job would have gone to someone else. He pushed the buff folder across the desk.

'This is Hendry's service record, sir.'

The Chief dragged his chair into the circle of light from the reading lamp. Smooth white hair and sagging neck belied eyes and mouth a generation younger. He hitched up neat blue sleeves with the expertise of a conjurer and spread the contents of the file in front of him. A clipped sheaf of typescript – memoranda scrawled on odd bits of paper – a few glossy prints. He selected one of them, considered it with the concentration of a woman threading a needle.

The high-powered lens had caught the scene in vivid detail. A man in Commando uniform stood knee-deep in the wreckage of exploded steel and concrete. His blackened face accentuated the wideness of his smiling mouth. He was spreading the first two fingers of his right hand in the V sign.

The Chief flicked the print back across the desk. His grizzled sprouts of eyebrows lifted.

'Posing like a bloody film star. What rank did he hold here?'

The tone was hardly encouraging. Yet it was part of a routine familiar to them both. For all Gaunt knew, a necessary part. First came the problem, then the criticism of whatever solution he offered. He reversed the print, displaying the Ministry of Information stamp on the back.

'Captain, sir. The Ministry wanted a picture of the raid. I imagine he's standing as he was told to stand. It's the first drop, mission complete and recover job his unit did in Denmark. Hendry was decorated.'

The Chief gave no sign of having heard. He read steadily through the typescript, muttering occasionally under his breath. Finally, he laid the open folder in his lap and swept the top of the desk into it.

'We've known one another too long to pull punches, George. I've been in this service seventeen years. We've always had leaks. Some bloody fool or other in a mess over women or drink. Then, God help us, the queers. These were all calculated risks – this is different. Take the figures. Berlin – seven key men lost in a month – none of them known to one another. In Vienna it's just as bad. Polz with his head in a gas oven, Reidermeister missing. Since the end of June, every move we've made in the area has been forestalled. And what have we been able to produce? – a composite description of a traitor that would fit me equally well as you.' He emptied his lungs with disgust.

Gaunt was spuriously cheerful. 'That's how it looks now, I'll agree. But a few more days will give us a much different picture.'

The Chief's stare gathered intensity. 'It better had. Bryant's been sending me chits like a pregnant housemaid. "The whole structure of policy in balance" – stuff like that. And I've got to face him tonight with the news that we propose to rely on a convicted thief to get us out of trouble. I hope he appreciates it.' He perched the file on his knee and opened it again.

The indignation left Gaunt unimpressed. No one knew better than this man that there was no alternative.

'Bryant's a politician, sir. He'll find virtue in any situation. He'll do whatever you say in spite of what he may really think. You could remind him that we've had eleven days to find someone fluent in German and capable of opening a safe. Someone with an incentive. If he suggests we didn't have to go outside the Service to find that, make it clear there's another requirement. Our man must be expendable.'

The Chief's neck reformed under a lifted chin.

'Don't you start to be touchy, George, for God's sake. I know this business leaves as bad a taste in your mouth as in mine. It's an indecent thought – a traitor among the chaps you serve with. And this bloke's clever. Unless he's found, he'll sit there laughing at us, biding his time till we've built up replacements. Then the whole thing repeats itself.' He pushed his chair back, his mouth self-derisive. 'I'm two stone overweight and a pledge of loyalty to the men this bastard is destroying. This is a personal issue. Does that filter into your dedicated head?'

Gaunt's nod was the only acknowledgement of a quick and secret stimulation. The word 'dedicated' lost meaning in its own sound. If this fat ageing man meant 'set apart for a special purpose', he was right.

'Suppose we accept his cleverness. Try to reason as he will. He knows that the field of suspects must be narrowed. The end result is as plain to him as to us. Fifteen names – all people who must have been in this room at one time or another – all fifteen equally guilty or innocent. Including ourselves.'

The Chief's eyes were the colour of starling's eggs.

'But now we can fit a face to one of those names, George. That's what gives me hope – our friend isn't as imaginative as he might be. We know his chums took insurance against future defection. They put this Hamburg meeting on film. The question is, does *he* know it?'

Gaunt stared straight into the light of the desk lamp. The clock on the mantel shuddered past the quarter hour, banging its cracked note hurriedly. He looked up.

'For the past week I've tried to ask as few questions as I could, sir. This one's important. How good is your source of information?'

The Chief gathered confidence. 'It's from your own territory, George – Dusseldorf. You know Manfred's record. He's been with us since nineteen forty-five. What better person to have working on your side than a cell leader – a card-carrying Party member from the early thirties. You know the history of the family. Without the brother's help, things in Berlin could have been worse. Whatever Manfred says, I'm ready to accept as gospel. The film was developed in Krefeld. They're being ultra cautious – nobody's had a chance to get near it. Within the next few days it will be delivered to the Bulgarian Ministry. How long it'll stay in their safe I don't yet know. This much is certain – out it goes in the diplomatic bag unless we get there first.'

Gaunt lifted his shoulders. 'Then you'll have to make up your mind about Hendry, sir.'

The Chief's voice was suddenly tired. 'There are times when you make me feel a doddering old fool, George. Very well. I've read his service record – I know he's a thief. What else is there?'

Gaunt was diffident. 'It's hard to say – I've only seen him in court. You could almost see the chip on his shoulder. There's no doubt of his professional competence.'

The Chief shut his eyes, speaking with feeling. 'Professional competence – God almighty! Well – once he's in, he's in, George. You realize the implications.'

Gaunt's answer had the same flat finality. 'I'm ready to take full responsibility for Hendry, sir. Before and after.'

The Chief nodded heavily. 'I suppose anything's better than sitting on your arse in a cell for years. You say he'll be sentenced tomorrow?'

Gaunt was on his feet. He started walking the width of the room, following a diagonal line in the carpet.

'I've kept clear of the Yard for obvious reasons but I do have a contact in the Criminal Records Office. I'm told the rumour there is that Hendry's innocent.'

The Chief leaned back, his whistle short and shrill. He put the question indulgently. 'You pose a neat exercise in ethics. Are you interested in that sort of thing?'

Gaunt stopped by the curtained window. 'At the moment I'm interested in anything that might affect Hendry's behaviour, sir. That's why I intend to find out who framed him and why.'

The Chief locked both hands behind his neck. 'Well, watch your step. I can handle the Commissioner of Police. The Home Office is another story. Don't fall foul of those buggers, George. We're going to have to ask them for help.'

Gaunt dropped back in his seat. The tension was gone. Anything he did would be supported to the limit of his superior's experience and authority.

'I've already been to the Home Office, sir. They're willing to co-operate. But the Permanent Secretary insists on a signature – preferably Bryant's.'

The Chief's smile was grim. 'He can certainly have that. It'll be a pleasure.'

It seemed the right moment for the next request. 'I'll need five thousand pounds available in Germany within the next two days, sir. Part of the deal with Hendry.'

His superior scribbled on a pad. 'I'm not given to ghoulishness but it occurs to me that he may not live to spend it. Just how much do you propose telling him?'

Gaunt's eyes were steady. 'Enough to give him a chance to go on living. I wouldn't say he's in a position to expect anything more.'

The big man hauled himself from his seat. He crossed the room to the white-painted cupboard and made a selection from the bottles in front of him. He dropped ice into gin and tonic water, humming. He spoke idly, his eyes curious as he held out the glass.

'They're good tunes, Hymns Ancient and Modern. Do you ever say your prayers, George?'

Gaunt watched the last bubble to the surface.

'Repeatedly, sir. As often as I'm in trouble, in fact. Why?'

The Chief raised his glass. 'Then you'd better get in a quick word for all of us. Especially for Hendry. To paraphrase the saying – as he goes, so goes the Service.' His smile held no real humour.

3

GAUNT PAID off the cab outside the Old Bailey. It was just ten as he climbed the steps to the main hall. The Public Gallery entrance was round the corner. The crowd here had more intimate concern with the business of the courts. It divided into wary groups of hard-eyed cops herding attentive witnesses; nervous defendants surrendering to their bail, flanked by tearful relatives; barristers with their instructing solicitors. Nobody spoke much. Faces were strained. Everyone watched the clock.

Gaunt rapped on the door of the office beside the telephone booths. He followed the police-sergeant's directions. Past the stern stone heads of forgotten judges, down the wide staircase to the labyrinth underneath the courtrooms. A few people were snatching last-minute cups of coffee in the cafeteria through the archway. A man in a rumpled suit sat at a corner table talking earnestly to a woman peaked with pregnancy. He smiled suddenly and shook the last of a pint bottle of Scotch into her tea cup.

The air was sour with fear and misery. A steel gate barred Gaunt's way to the cells. He pressed the bell on the wall. The warder who answered wore a cap heavy with gold braid — a ponderous man, still digesting his breakfast and suspicious.

'Christopher Hendry? No, sir. Nobody's allowed down here without a court order.' He inspected Gaunt's black jacket, striped trousers and briefcase. 'You're not his solicitor, are you?'

Gaunt showed the Board of Trade pass. It bore a name and his picture.

'If there's any difficulty get in touch with the Deputy-Governor of the prison. He'll vouch for me.'

The man replaced caution with deference. 'That's all right, sir. I didn't get the name.' The steel gates swung open. He led the way, waddling like a king penguin along a corridor lined with cells and smelling of carbolic. The passage widened into a bay lit by naked bulbs. Another warder was sitting on a chair by the steps leading to the court. He struggled up, buttoning his tunic.

'Eleven men, all correct, sir.'

The Principal Officer touched his cap in acknowledgement. 'Thank you, Mr Rowlands. Unlock Hendry for a visit.' He showed Gaunt the door facing them. 'I'll put you in the Solicitors' Room, sir. You'll be nice and private. You know the rules, I expect. In sight and out of hearing, that's how we work. You're not allowed to give anything to the prisoner or receive anything from him.'

Gaunt threw his briefcase on the table. He glanced casually through the glass windows to the corridor.

'I understand perfectly, officer. This is purely a routine investigation but I may need to see this man again afterwards. Would that be in order?'

The warder consulted an old-fashioned watch. 'Better for me, sir. I can't let you keep him too long now. He's first on the list for sentence. A quarter of an hour's the limit.' He rolled away to his post and matters of more interest.

The air down here was a stale relic of yesterday. There was none of the open tension of the scene outside the court-room. Remorse and rebellion were decently confined behind cell doors. He felt furtively under the polished wood surface of the table. The tiled walls and light fixture looked innocent enough. The clerk at the Home Office had been emphatic – almost indignant at Gaunt's inquiry. Certainly none of the interview rooms at the Old Bailey was equipped with recording devices. Footsteps sounded. Gaunt raised his head.

The man coming towards him was squinting against the brightness of the light. He stood uncertainly, his back to the closing door. A little taller than average, lean in a grey flannel suit.

Gaunt pointed at the empty chair. 'Sit down, Hendry.'

The briefcase on the table held a dozen pictures of this man. He could have catalogued each feature from memory. The wide mouth over a stubborn chin – the short nose scarred across the bridge. The colour of the hair had changed from brown to grey. Only the expression of the eyes had defeated the camera. No lens could convey this look of implacable mistrust.

He offered the pack of cigarettes, ignoring the warder patrolling the corridor.

'We don't have much time. The first thing you must understand is that I'm not a policeman. I'm concerned with your special abilities not your morals.'

Hendry rolled the fat Turkish cigarette between his fingers. He was neither hostile nor encouraging. 'My special abilities! Which ones?'

Gaunt searched ineffectually for a light. Hendry passed

half a match across the table, his mouth sardonic as Gaunt struggled with the flaming sliver.

'You're going into court in a few minutes,' said Gaunt. 'I'm told you'll get ten years. Is this what you expect?'

Hendry's eyes widened. He tapped the short ash from his cigarette, his expression thoughtful.

'You say you're not a cop. All right, I'll buy that. A reporter wouldn't get by the gate. That leaves some sort of quack? At a guess I'd say a psychologist. I've been through this before, doctor. I don't have any guilt complex. In fact, my behaviour is supposed to be typically psychopathic in its refusal of guilt. You see, I do know the game. The bit with the ink-blots, everything. I never felt rejected by my mother and I learned about sex from a doctor's daughter. We were both eighteen and approved of it. It's nice talking to you but you're wasting your time.'

Gaunt ignored the defiant irony. 'A few years ago, you burgled a house where eleven people and three dogs were sleeping. You took the keys of the safe from underneath Benurian's pillow and stole thirty thousand pounds in negotiable securities. Is that an accurate description of your performance?'

Hendry nodded easily. 'Very accurate indeed. It makes me revise my first guess. You're from the insurance company and you want to know what happened to the bonds. I'll tell you. I cashed them in and went to live in Brazil. In fact I'm still living the good life there. A little ashamed, maybe, but with no real cares. Now let me out of here.' He pushed his chair back.

Gaunt kept his temper, creating a building in the air with his fingers. 'This is a house a few miles out of a large German city. Not unlike the one you robbed five years ago. It's set in wooded country off the *autobahn*. It's never empty and there's a Mark IV Bode safe in one of the rooms. How would you assess the chances of opening that safe and getting away with it?'

Hendry used his heel to stamp the last glow from the cigarette butt. His tone was still pleasant.

'I thought you guys earned good money. You know your trouble – you mix with the wrong people.' He made as if to rise.

Gaunt shoved the table forward, pinning the Canadian on a teetering chair. 'Don't be a fool. The right answer can save you.'

Hendry recovered his balance, finding the floor with a rueful smile. 'I smell the doctor again. I'm half inclined to report you to the British Medical Association. You're a head case yourself. But I'll give you something for your notebook. A Bode Mark IV is a wall safe. It has a quarter-inch tungsten face that is heat resistant. If you didn't have the key and knew how, you could blow the box out the window and be on the street before it landed. That's more or less the answer, isn't it?'

Gaunt's eyes were fixed on the strong bitter face. 'Would you like a chance to prove that statement?'

Hendry's mouth opened slightly. He wet the edges of his lips cautiously. His reply came in a whisper.

'Just what are you getting at?'

The warder stopped at the door. He looked at his watch and gave them two minutes. Gaunt made each word tell.

'This is serious. What happens upstairs in the court doesn't have to mean a thing. I want you to open a safe for me. If you bring it off, there'll be five thousand pounds and your freedom. A ticket to anywhere in the world. You think it over. I'll see you after you're sentenced. And keep your mouth shut.'

He walked behind Hendry and tapped on the glass. 'I haven't quite finished here, warder. I'll have to come back again after he's been into court.'

The man grinned. 'He won't be going far, sir.'

The judge was already sitting when Gaunt slipped into Court Number One. The Board of Trade pass was good for a seat behind the glass-screened dock. The group of reporters, the detectives at their table – offered no more than token interest as defence counsel came to his feet. For the initiated, the drama had hit its peak with the jury's verdict. As Cameron started his speech, Hendry turned his head slightly, looking around the court. He met Gaunt's glance without any sign of recognition.

Cameron made his plea with quietness and feeling.

'My lord – a man of forty-three years of age has been convicted in this court as a habitual criminal. We have heard him described as dangerous and determined. These are what a jury has held to be the facts in this case – the sum total of a man's life and endeavour. It is no flight of fancy to say that an assessment of this kind is incomplete. Can any one of us here today hope for judgement without compassion and understanding? Let me show you a young man of twenty-one, standing on the threshold of an orderly, prosperous life. In a few months he will be the possessor of a degree marking an academic career of distinction. Then comes war. Those of us old enough to remember those first dark days when this island stood alone will not easily forget the feeling of pride as one after another member of our great Commonwealth answered the call. Still less do we forget the arrival of the Vanguard – the First Canadian Division. Some young – some less young – but every man a volunteer, submerging self-interest in a common cause.'

He drank water unhurriedly.

'I need not remind you that the waging of war requires those who are led and those who must lead. Of these last something more than obedience is required. "Dangerous and determined!" Surely these were the very qualities that must be marked and fostered – the stuff that made men brave in the face of the enemy and devoted to their duty? We judged Hendry then and were grateful. But we have grown cynical – aloof from the rebel we ourselves created. M'lord – with all the respect and sincerity at my command I submit we are wrong. I am an officer of this court, pledged to uphold its noble traditions. Yet I ask for more than leniency – I ask for understanding. I ask you to commit Hendry to the care of those persons qualified to give him the psychological help he needs. Twenty-two years ago he made a decision that imperilled his future – he made it in the name of humanity.

I ask your lordship to do as much today.' He sat down, wiping his neck, eyes fixed on the water bottle in front of him.

The judge waited for the last cough to be smothered. He watched Hendry stand and spoke without passion – as if conscious of being the mouthpiece of an infallible principle.

'I'm not going to waste time or words, Hendry. This is the fourth occasion on which you have been found guilty of a serious crime. I have listened sympathetically to the devoted plea made on your behalf. I find in it no valid excuse for what amounts to an overt and persistent defiance of the law. No battle record, however courageous, affords licence to the individual to carry on a personal war against Society. Not once have you expressed regret for your conduct. Indeed, I sense in your demeanour an indifference to the opinion of decent people. You shall have ample time to ponder it. You will go to Preventive Detention for a term of twelve years.'

Gaunt pushed his way along the row, stumbling in his haste. Downstairs, the same warder let him through the passgate and into the Solicitors' Room. It was only minutes before Hendry was ushered in. The Canadian sat down heavily, pale and shaken. He took the cigarette Gaunt offered, fumbling with a light.

Gaunt spoke quietly. Instinct told him that sympathy was out of place.

'Have you made up your mind?'

Hendry seemed to have difficulty answering. 'Just who are you?'

Gaunt shrugged. 'An inspector of weights and measures attached to the Board of Trade. That'll have to do. Now listen – your freedom depends on learning a few essentials very quickly. First is the need to keep your mouth closed and not ask questions. Every bargain needs a basis of agreement. I want your word that you'll honour your side of the deal.'

Hendry's clasped hands obscured his face. 'Twelve stinking years,' he said slowly. 'Did you get the look in his eyes as he said it? I'm dead, man. Finished.'

Gaunt spoke soothingly. He had the feeling that this man's allegiance would be entire. It was not yet pledged.

'You're nowhere near finished, Hendry. This isn't a trick. If you're ready to co-operate, you'll be out of prison in a few days. Nobody in this building knows who I am or why I've seen you – still less the judge.'

Hendry sat up straight. The colour was returning to his cheeks. He took a deep breath.

'I wouldn't care if you were Hitler. Get me out of here and you make your own terms.'

There was a scuffle outside. A couple of warders wrestled a shouting man from the dock to his cell. The door slammed on the last obscene abuse.

Gaunt tapped his briefcase. 'They're simple enough. I've got your Canadian passport in here. You'll be issued with another travel document. We're both realists, Hendry. You're not going to take offence when I say I've tried putting myself in your place. You see, you're my responsibility. Welsh on the bargain and I'll take care of you personally. There's one thing about your army record nobody mentioned. You never liked discipline. That's what I'll expect. Complete obedience.'

Hendry's face reddened. 'I never broke my word. In the army or out of it.'

The show of indignation left Gaunt undisturbed. 'Possibly not. That's beside the point, anyway. We're conspirators in a sense, Hendry. Mutual advantage links us. I'm an improviser. I have to use whatever tools I can lay my hands on. There's always a natural hope that they'll be dependable. But still take precautions against disappointment. Am I making myself clear?'

The Canadian's eyes were steady. 'Very clear. But don't think I'll believe all this sitting in a cell in Wandsmoor Prison.'

Gaunt collected his hat and briefcase. It was just as well this man didn't realize his own importance. He stood up.

'You'll believe it. Your job starts the moment you leave this room. The prison authorities will know nothing. I've repeated this because it's important. In a few days you'll be told that you're being temporarily released for psychiatric treatment. Your barrister's plea couldn't have been more fortunate. We're going to be seeing a lot of one another, Hendry.

I suggest that you spend the time to our next meeting trying to understand precisely what this will mean. Obedience. There's one last thing. I think you're too sensible to confide in anyone else. Loose talk ruins you not me.'

4

THE EAST WIND blew in gusts, driving the hail against the two houses making a dead-end of the short street. Bernadette Jeffries moved away from the window as a man turned the far corner. She hurried to the square gilt mirror in the hall, a hint of North American Indian in the slashed red mouth, high-bridged nose and coarse black hair. A smear of Vaseline on the lids heightened the brilliance of her black eyes.

The outline of a man's figure showed through the glass street door. He was standing beneath the hanging lamp. She had turned the handle before he had time to press the bell push.

He came in, touching her cheek with cold fingers. She shook the wet from his trench coat and followed him into the sitting-room. When she had drawn the grey tweed curtains, shutting out the gathering dusk, she turned to face him.

'I was beginning to worry. What kept you so long, Philip?'

Proctor was in his late thirties with smooth fair hair and the mouth of a dissenter. His blue hopsack jacket hung from heavy shoulders. He carried himself lazily, legs elegant in narrow trousers, as far as the trolley and poured himself a drink. He propped his seat on the arm of the sofa, baring his teeth at the bitterness of the lemon. He swirled the glass a couple of times then looked up at her.

'I thought I asked you not to ring me at home. It was pure luck I answered the phone and not my mother. Otherwise . . .' he made a gesture of someone being run through the front door – 'What are you trying to do – make sure I get thrown out?'

She arranged long legs under her. The bracelet on her

wrist was heavy. She undid the catch and laid the coiled gold in her lap.

'You make it difficult for me to understand you, Philip. Do you really think I'd deliberately do anything to harm you?'

He fished a lump of ice from his drink and threw it into the fireplace.

'Let me tell you something – my mother provides me with food and a bed. She's made her conditions. Staying away from you is one of them. It's no life for me but it's the best I can do. The day I find myself lining up in front of the Salvation Army hostel, I'm going to be concerned with results not reasons. Let's take it from there.'

She was unable to keep the resentment from her voice. 'If I'd known anywhere else to call, don't you think I'd have preferred that? But it's three weeks since I've seen you, remember. This is an emergency.'

He hoisted his glass in her direction, smiling gravely. 'God Almighty, but that sounds familiar! Have you any idea how many times I've heard the same thing? The day you thought Hendry saw us at the races. The day he got pinched. Even the night he was sentenced. I've never been able to work out what you mean by an emergency.'

'Haven't you? It's not too difficult. All it takes is to imagine yourself in trouble and in need of help. In jail, for instance, and without the price of a lawyer.'

He kicked a log to a blaze and hid the fire with his legs. He was no longer smiling.

'Isn't that a long way below the belt?'

She came to her feet. 'They're your rules. I don't even like them.'

He nodded, his eyes brooding. 'But you still want to punish me, is that it? A QC to defend me – seeing you every month. Then the weekends together when it was all over. All paid for with another man's money. I haven't been grateful enough. Is that what sticks in your gizzard?'

She shook her head. From the beginning she had known he mistrusted any show of strength in a woman. Her own

22

had always been hidden. For two years she had struggled to hold him, using what means she might. Two years, lying to another man she no longer cared for. Every hour desperate with her fear of detection. What stuck in her gizzard was that when there was no longer any reason for fear, Proctor had gone home to his mother.

'If there's nothing else going,' she said steadily, 'I prefer loyalty to gratitude.'

He smiled again, suddenly and as if he meant it. 'Why you picked on me I'll never know. But I'm glad.'

She closed her eyes as he came towards her. Then the warmth of his hands was on her throat, the tangy roughness of his cheek against her. All her life she had fought for what she wanted. This would be no different.

She pulled herself free and searched the bureau drawer for the cheap white envelope. The address was scrawled in Hendry's writing.

> Mrs Bernadette Jeffries,
> 11 Chivers Street,
> SW3

She handed the letter to Proctor. 'I didn't call you for nothing – this came in the afternoon mail.'

The lined paper was headed Wandsmoor Prison. It bore a cell number and censor's stamp. Proctor read through the two short paragraphs, inspected the blank back page and returned the letter.

'Very touching. What about it?'

'Read it out loud,' she insisted, 'then tell me what you think.'

He swallowed the last of his drink and read, running one sentence into another without expression or intonation.

Dearest Bernadette,

By now I hope you'll have heard from the bank. Your signature's all that's necessary. The money I've managed to rake up doesn't seem much but I have the feeling that it will be enough.

So far I've been sleeping well – a contented mind, I guess. God knows I miss you but even that situation isn't without hope. Take care of yourself and don't bother to write.

I'm crazy about you,
Kit.

He tossed the sheet back to her. 'What am I supposed to say? I don't know how his mind works. Don't you realize I played hide-and-seek for two years with a man I never laid eyes on? I haven't even seen a picture of him. I'd say he sounds too bloody cheerful for a man doing twelve years, but that's his business. Possibly he knows when he's well off.'

She pulled the tartan dress over slim silk knees, frowning. 'I've lived with Kit on and off for nine years. I understand every thought process in that Scotch-Presbyterian head as well as my own. Sometimes better. This letter is phoney, Philip. He had it all worked out, the last time he went to jail. A man in prison had no right to a woman. He said it again when he came out. There'd be no more waiting around for me to do. This letter's completely out of character. I'm going to tell you something. If I were the nervous type, I'd be looking in cupboards by now.'

He collapsed on the sofa, head and neck deep in the cushions, staring at the ceiling.

'What have you got to be afraid of? You needn't worry about me. I'm not an embarrassment. Anyway, what friends has he got to run round corners after you? He's a dead member. In a month or so, he'll be buried in some maximum security prison. And good luck to him. Did you ever hear from the bank?'

She saw something young in his mouth as he sprawled. She wanted to freeze the pose, to keep him there, relaxed and dependent. Rather than see him pull away, she resisted the impulse to touch him. He had a cat's indifference to a caress.

She answered indulgently. 'He must have been holding out. The bank says he had a credit of seven hundred pounds. Why is he suddenly so generous? This may sound crazy, Philip, but I have the feeling Kit's planning on breaking jail. If it means enough to him, he'll do it. Suppose the answer's money – a lot of money – hidden where only he can get at it?'

He considered her lazily with pale blue eyes. 'What money? You've been telling me for the last year that he was pleading poverty. He got away with nothing this time.'

His sudden interest amused and flattered her. 'Money that you know nothing about. Five years ago Kit went to jail for stealing thirty thousand pounds' worth of securities. There was a man in Germany who was going to negotiate them. Then he backed out at the last moment. Kit always claimed that he burned the securities. But suppose he was lying – suppose he'd kept those stock certificates all this time. And just when he's on the point of turning them into money, the police arrest him. Wouldn't that be a good enough reason for breaking jail?'

Proctor was watching her guardedly. 'It might give him a reason but there's a trained staff dedicated to the idea of keeping him where he is. He won't be able to move a yard without a screw breathing down his neck. And without outside help what chance would he have? Who's going to stick out his neck for a has-been?'

She was suddenly impatient with his lack of vision. He knew nothing of the nerveless desperation that drove Hendry into disregard of danger.

'We are,' she said quietly.

He almost choked on the implication. 'You're insane, Bernadette. Stark, raving mad! What could we do?'

Her dark eyes were thoughtful. 'Kit trusts me. There's only one thing that would have kept him from telling me about the money. He'd be scared of involving me in the risk. What if I disregard this letter and go to see him – tell him I want to get him out of jail? I'll know the truth just as soon as I look at his face.'

Proctor flexed his arms, his mouth uneasy. 'Has he ever tried breaking jail before? If he has he'll be on the Escape List. That means he'd have no chance.'

She answered impatiently. 'Kit's not a fool. He's never

25

tried to run. He never had to.' She was on her feet and dialling the phone before Proctor could stop her.

He stood across the room, not missing a word of what she was saying. When she was done, he filled her empty glass. She wriggled her shoulders.

'Well, that's that. His solicitor says I won't be allowed to see him for a month. But I've got to know, Philip.'

He brought the tips of black polished shoes together, looking down at them as though they might offer inspiration.

'You can wait a month,' he said slowly. 'Until then you've got to keep him where he is – behaving himself.'

He carried paper from the writing desk and put it by her side.

'Get hold of that pen,' he instructed. He walked from fireplace to wall and back, dictating as he went.

'"Dearest – Darling" whatever it is you call him – "Kit. Your letter made me very happy, at the same time a little sad. I'm afraid my nights haven't been as peaceful as yours. It isn't easy to tell you how much I miss and need you – I can't help remembering a censor has to read this letter. The shock of your sentence made me sick for two days. All I could do was lie here in an empty house, remembering the misery of our last months together. The stupid, pointless quarrels, all the time realizing how much of the blame was mine. You said in your letter not to write – how *couldn't* I, Kit! I had to tell you that I shared your hope – to tell you about my own – to beg of you *not* to make any decision that will affect us both until after I've visited you. I know just how you feel about me seeing you in prison but this time it's necessary. There's something you've got to know that I can't put in writing."'

He nibbled the back of a finger. 'Sign it and I'll drop it in the box on my way out.'

She licked the flap on the envelope, watching him carefully.

'I never wrote him a letter like that in my life. It sounds as though I'm getting ready to knit little garments.'

Proctor nodded. 'All the better. It'll keep him where he is

until you go to see him.' He stretched easily and sat down yawning.

'Mother's alone tonight. I'd better put in an appearance. Cold beef and Spanish burgundy. Ah well.'

She put down her glass and crossed the room. She took the hand he extended, held it against her breast. The thinning patch on his scalp was plain from above. It would have been the same to her if he hadn't a hair on his head.

'The hell with your mother,' she said deliberately. 'Would you tolerate a divorced woman for the night? A very affectionate divorced woman?'

He grinned up at her, opening his eyes wide. 'Do you know, I just might – especially if she offered me a meal as well.' He pulled her down to him, finding the hollow in her neck with his mouth.

5

HENDRY WOKE after the worst night since he'd emptied his pockets on the desk in the Reception Wing office. For too long he'd lain on the bed, waiting for the padding footsteps of the night patrol. The click of the spyhole – the creak of the door as the man's weight tested the lock. Then all the lights had gone out and he'd been alone with the troubled sounds of a jail at sleep.

He no longer punished himself with the memory of betrayal and injustice. To quote Cameron, those were the facts. The facts that had produced a foxy-faced stranger in a black coat and striped trousers. Seventy-two hours had passed since then but every inflection of the man's voice was clear. Clear, too, the indifference with which he had demolished jail walls and judge, offering freedom in their place. At night in the darkness, the picture was brilliant. In the light of day and the sordid drudgery of prison routine it faded to a meaningless blur.

Now it was morning. The bell above the chapel tolled

nine o'clock with dismal finality. Beyond the door, the cell block banged and clattered into activity. He shook the crumbs from his plate cloth on to the window ledge, put his library books and card on the table for changing and stood by his door. Here you lived by your ears. Prompted by bells, shouts, and the clashing of keys in locks. The screw's tread along the landing was heavy. That would be Burgess and a rough time in the shop today. Four steps took the jailer from cell to cell. There was a pause as he looked for a misplaced chamber pot, untidy bedding. That flatfooted herald of yet another day to be crossed off the calendar. Only this morning for some reason the summons missed Hendry. He heard the rest of the gallery unlocked.

He sat nervously on his chair, listening to the landing orderly's dreary Irish dirge. After a quarter of an hour came the sound of more footsteps – the scrape of wood along the wall as someone inspected his cell card. The door was thrown open. The young screw's face was unfamiliar. He checked Hendry's name and number against the list he was holding.

'Going out tomorrow, aren't you? Go down and wait on the end of A2. You'll be for the SMO first and then the Governor.'

For a moment Hendry stayed in his place, frozen to disbelief. Surely the screw would be back in a couple of minutes to correct his mistake. But the jailer was already on the next landing, unlocking another man due for discharge. The relaxed surveillance was significant. As though a watch kept on someone with one foot through the Main Gate would be pointless. Hendry hauled himself up, moving as if he were half stunned. He held his water jug in shaking hands and drank till his stomach revolted. He made his way along the gallery, down the spiral stairs to the brilliantly lighted Centre. Here was the core of the jail – a round glass edifice like a Paris street kiosk stripped of its newspapers. It was the hub from which the five cell blocks radiated, each with its five tiers of galleries. Ten feet above Hendry's head stretched the suicide-proof netting. He skirted the edge of stone flagging that was never quite dry and never completely wet. Generations of cons in kneeling pads had crept backwards over this floor dragging buckets of cold water after them. A stench of disinfectant and excrement pervaded the whole building.

He took his place on the end of the queue. Every man on the line from where he stood to the Senior Medical Officer's door carried the excitement of impending freedom with him. The pair of hands on front of Hendry gripped and twisted behind it's owner's back. An old man with a white cane hung his head, carefully averting his dim sight and secret smile from the working party that tramped by. Everyone here was a member of an exclusive club with a long waiting list. Hendry heard his name called. He followed the Hospital Orderly into the room.

The doctor was reading a medical record. He raised his head, bristle browed and interested.

'Well, Hendry, it looks as though we're losing you.'

Hendry shuffled in broken-heeled shoes, trying to look decently surprised. 'Yes, doctor.'

The Medical Officer turned the pages of the record curiously. 'Shut the door, will you, Mr Parks? Take off your shirt and drop your trousers, Hendry.'

Cold fingers explored the Canadian's body. He inhaled and exhaled, hearing the thud of his heart under the stethoscope. The skin beneath his eyes was dragged down. His legs jerked from sharp blows under his kneecaps. The doctor's pen scratched busily as Hendry put his clothes on again.

'Nothing much wrong with you, is there?' he asked conversationally. 'Your heart and lungs are ten years younger than you are – did you know that?'

Hendry wriggled into the battledress top. 'I suppose I've kept fairly good shape, doctor.' The words sounded false – the wrong answer in a game he only half understood. Even now he expected a sudden blast to strip his pretence.

The doctor's face brooded over his papers. 'You know why you're being released – the Prison Commissioners are giving you a chance in a million to help yourself. Medicine can do only so much for people like you, Hendry. Most of it'll be up to yourself. I've gone through the report of your case very carefully. Do you still maintain that you're innocent?'

Hendry knew the answer expected. He shook his head.

'No, doctor.'

The Medical Officer closed the record in front of him. 'Then you're beginning to show sense. Good luck.'

The Canadian made no reply. The Hospital Orderly was holding the door open. Hendry went out, facing the last hurdle between him and the winning post. He joined the queue outside the Governor's office. This was a less distinguished line. An assembly of 'call-ups' – the jail jargon for those summoned to hear some special piece of information from the official mouth. The news might be trite or dramatic. The stereotyped reply to a petition – 'The Home Secretary has fully considered your request but is unable to grant it.' A Dear John letter from a delinquent wife – or the pompous rhetoric reserved for men due for release the following day.

The door to the Governor's office was hurled back. The warder used the strangled bawl dear to army sweats.

'3467 Hendry, sir! Stand to attention on the white line and give your full name to the Governor.'

The man behind the desk wore civilian clothes and his hat. The Chief Officer standing at his right shoulder whipped Hendry's prison record in front of his superior. The Governor scanned the slip pinned on its front. He cleared his throat, seeming to have difficulty framing his words.

'I have a Home Office order here for your release on parole, Hendry. You'll be told when and where to report when you sign the necessary papers. Are there any questions?'

Hendry's mouth was dry again. For three days and nights he'd swung between doubt and certainty. Wherever he'd gone, cell, workshop, or exercise yard, Gaunt's face had accompanied him. Thin, hard, and compelling. He'd been lucky to lock up alone. Seventy-five per cent of the jail population was housed three in a cell. Only the length of his sentence had ensured his privacy. The pure mechanics of freedom offered no problem. The Home Secretary had the power to release any prisoner. He'd done it in war time – Why not now if Gaunt's promise was valid? If not, there were four thousand days ahead with no certainty of remission, the last no better than the first. If he lived that long he'd be over fifty when he came out. Broke and forgotten.

'No questions,' he answered quietly.

The Chief Officer's face reddened. 'Say "sir" when you address the Governor.'

It was a fair enough comment. Certainly you were supposed to approach God with reverence. 'Sir,' he added hastily.

The man behind the desk turned his full attention on the Canadian. He seemed to take the situation as a personal affront.

'There's nothing in your medical history to suggest mental aberration. You've always been marked A1 for labour. What *is* all this nonsense about?'

Hendry was particularly respectful. 'I honestly don't know, sir. I can only suppose it has something to do with my lawyer. He asked for psychological treatment at my trial. That's all I can think of.'

The Governor leaned both elbows on the desk, punctuating his words with his pen. His mouth was sour and disparaging.

'I'm going to tell you something for your own good. This isn't a discharge. It's a temporary release on parole. Step out of line and you'll be back here growing old in the service. They're used to leadswingers at Millbank Hospital. You won't find it so easy to fox the doctors there.' The thought apparently cheered him. He turned to the Chief Officer. 'What's this man's behaviour like since he's been admitted?'

Hendry composed himself to patience. As long as the roll call was right it was no concern of either man whether he lived or died. But the farce still had to be played out. The implicit threat acknowledged that his liberty somehow depended on his good behaviour and their grace.

The Chief Officer took a good look at Hendry for the first time in his life. He made a show of considering judgement. 'I've had no complaints about him, sir.'

The Governor heard the news without enthusiasm.

'Get out,' he said suddenly.

31

The young warder who had unlocked Hendry was waiting on the Centre. He crooked his finger at the Canadian.

'Fetch your towel and soap for a bath. Make it lively. It might be a long time before you get another one, mate.'

It was a quarter to eight in the Reception Wing. A bleary-eyed cleaner pushed a broom listlessly at the debris of the previous night. Hendry walked into the office. The Chief Officer wore authority like another campaign ribbon. He shook out the small bag, checking each article against the property sheet on the top of the desk.

'One pair of cuff links. One wristlet watch. A wallet with various papers and four photographs. One fountain pen. Three pounds, fourteen shillings and sixpence cash.'

Hendry scrawled his name at the foot of the sheet. The prison uniform lay in a heap in the cubicle outside. His own grey flannel suit seemed without weight – the silk shirt soft on his skin. The three other men due for discharge that morning were already gone. He stood attentively as the Chief read from the parole paper.

'I suppose you know what being on your honour means? You'll leave here without an escort and report to the Millbank Hospital at half past nine this morning. Is that clear?'

'Quite clear.'

The Chief Officer pushed an envelope across the desk.

'This letter came for you this morning. Do you want to make any complaints about your treatment here before you go, Hendry?'

The bold, square handwriting was familiar. He put the envelope in an inside pocket.

'I've no complaints, sir.'

It was barely daylight as the gatekeeper unlocked the wicket in the massive studded doors. One step took Hendry into the forecourt. He hurried towards the trees as if even now a shout might recall him. The last of the night fog clung to slippery bare branches – covered the car in front of the Governor's house with a damp, lustreless film. He read Bernadette's letter carefully, ripped it in pieces and dumped them in a litter bin. The bus stop was a hundred yards away. He flagged down the first double decker and rode it as far as Clapham Junction. He stood on the corner, wearing his freedom uneasily – as if he carried some sign that set him apart from the hurrying crowds on their way to work.

He bought a newspaper and read the headlines. Strike, scandal, and crisis. Nothing had changed. Time seemed to have been suspended since the night the squad car roared into the mews where he lived. He crossed the street to the empty booth and dialled a Flaxman number. The insistent shrilling went unanswered. He put the receiver down, his mouth indulgent, remembering black tousled hair pressed into a pillow. Bernadette slept long. It was not yet eight thirty. He'd try again later.

Another bus took him as far as the north Embankment. He walked towards Westminster, every block he passed a memory and a promise. The riverside club where they'd celebrated his birthday – a table overlooking water cool under the lavender haze of a summer evening. The squat museum, a reminder of echoing rooms hung with paintings where they'd sat hand in hand. Somewhere outside, a couple of cops had waited with a warrant. That was more than five years ago. These last few months something had driven a wedge between him and Bernadette, every blow of the hammer splitting them farther apart. The weeks before his arrest had been a misery of misunderstanding. It took a jail sentence to work out the uncomplicated truth. Never had he given Bernadette the one thing a woman wanted – the right to see him go and come without fear. The answer was simple. His freedom belonged to her. It had been a pretty hopeless realization, sitting in a cell. Now it had meaning again.

He found a small café near the hospital and sat staring through the steamed windows.

A few miles away, the punishment factory would be running at speed. The men who had been convicted with him at the Old Bailey were still there, pushing needles through mailbags stiff with the spittle and filth of countless railroad stations. Somehow he had been freed from the ordered nightmare. The feeling of unreality was still strong – as if he were on the run with no right to liberty. There was the same fear of danger from an unpredictable source. The man who came towards you with a smile was as much a threat as a blast from a police whistle. The parole paper had been ominous in its omissions. He was free for as little or as long as the Fate Sisters decided.

He left a coin beside the cup of stewed tea and went out to the street. The Enquiry Desk in the hospital lobby was open for business. A girl took his name. He watched the scrubbed sensible fingers pull a card from a file.

'There we are, Mr Hendry. You want Room 707, Doctor Ferguson.'

She indicated the direction he must take. Painted arrows led him along sterile passages, past operating theatres where angry red eyes glowed warning. Electronically controlled doors swung open at his approach. Finally he was in a hall flanked by offices. 707 was in the corner. Under the chromed numerals was a card in a slot.

Doctor Paul Ferguson.

He rapped tentatively on the door. It opened. A thickset man blocked the way. It was impossible to see round him. Hendry nodded.

'I have an appointment with Doctor Ferguson. My name's Christopher Hendry.'

The man pushed by without answering. As Hendry moved into the room, he heard the key turned and removed from the outside. The furnishings were few. A couple of chairs, a metal desk and file, a few text books. Gaunt was sitting on the horse-hair sofa against the far wall, swinging his legs. He wore a brown tweed suit with stout country shoes. His reddish hair was pulled forward so that it dipped over his forehead. His face seemed to have taken on an unfamiliar heartiness in keeping with his clothes. His voice was unchanged.

'Sit down. I'm glad to see you're punctual. How do you feel?'

'As though I'd been hit on the head,' Hendry said frankly. 'I'm still expecting someone to tap me on the shoulder – you know – "Back where you belong, bum!"'

Gaunt produced the fat silver cigarette case.

'Tell me something, Hendry. You wrote a letter to a Mrs Bernadette Jeffries three days ago. This morning you had an answer. I've seen copies of both.'

Hendry steadied himself for the right reply. 'Wasn't I supposed to write letters?'

Gaunt sniffed on the thought. 'Not without me knowing what you're up to.'

Fear hit like a blow from a fist. Hendry heard his own voice, very loud. 'She's a friend – a good friend. Isn't that enough?'

Gaunt still swung his legs easily. 'It may be for you. My approach is less emotional. Besides that, you're forgetting something. You don't have the right to any personal feelings, not until I'm done with you. And from my point of view they're highly dangerous. Are we together on that?'

Hendry's tongue loosened. The old black rage pumped his heart too fast. He shifted his weight cautiously. Gaunt not only called the dance, he invented the steps as you went along.

'We're reaching the stage when I ask myself whether what you're offering is any better than a cell.'

Gaunt cracked a pastille between his teeth, permeating the small room with the smell of peppermint. 'I thought you'd already answered that one. What's the matter, Hendry – can't you do what you're told even for a week? It's a fair enough exchange – that against twelve years' clink. All I'm asking is for you to play the game.'

Hendry looked open amazement. 'You're not expecting to be taken seriously with that "play the game" routine, are you?'

Gaunt's gesture was one of deprecation. 'Clichés. Someone always pins your ears back with them. You know perfectly well what I mean. I asked for unquestioning obedience – you promised it. Time enough for luxuries later.'

'Just what do you call luxuries?' Hendry said steadily.

Gaunt's expression was innocent. 'Establishing contact with people you know. Using me as a means of clearing your name. That sort of thing.'

It was hard to hide his disbelief. This man was a realist yet even he couldn't see the absurdity of the suggestion. Clear his name – as if guilt or innocence mattered to a guy in a spot like his. The essence was liberty. Once you had it, there was no time for ethical frills.

'I see,' he said slowly. 'Is there anything else I'm supposed to forget – like God or breathing?'

Gaunt was looking almost cheerful. 'If I think of anything else, I'll let you know. In the meantime tell me how this strikes you.' He pushed a paper at Hendry.

The passport application form had already been completed. The physical characteristics matched his own in detail. The name on the paper was Christopher Hendrik, born eleventh August, nineteen eighteen.

Gaunt nodded. 'That's near enough to your own name to cover you if you're caught off guard. The important thing is for you to believe in all this. You're described as a journalist – I'll leave it to you to think of a reason that would take you to Germany. Choose a subject you can talk about if you have to. Is there anything there that's worrying you?'

Hendry walked as far as the window. Beyond the tops of the bare trees along the Embankment, a wintry sun struck oily colour from the low tide mudbanks. Behind the spires of the Parliament buildings was New Scotland Yard. The progress of a file in the Criminal Record Office was inevitable. Once convicted, you could spend the rest of your life preaching the Gospel – your fingerprints still belonged in one of three categories. Active – Inactive – or Dead.

He turned his back on the picture. 'I'm giving up guessing who or what you are – one thing's sure – you've really gone to work on me, haven't you? As soon as I sign this form, you've got me for something else. Making a false statement to procure a passport. Do you really want to hear what's worrying me? Your lack of imagination! I've known Bernadette Jeffries for nine years. What harm can I do seeing her?'

Gaunt studied the fuzz on the back of his hand.

'I prefer to put it this way. There's nothing you could say that would satisfy a woman's curiosity – we'd better leave it at that. I want you to go and have some pictures done. Sign Doctor Ferguson's name on the back as sponsor. There's no danger. If you get to the passport office before noon, they'll deal with your application right away.'

Hendry put the paper in his wallet. There was nothing in Gaunt's head but a series of orders and responses. It was a waste of time looking for understanding. He held out his hand, displaying the three pound notes. 'All that takes money. This is what I'm worth.'

Gaunt felt in his pocket and produced an envelope.

'Ten pounds. Five hundred D marks and a ticket to Dusseldorf. Your flight leaves London Airport at quarter past eight tomorrow morning – Lufthansa.'

Hendry sat down again. Sunlight slanted across the polished linoleum, lightening the small bare room. He was already airborne, the last glimpse of England hidden by cloud.

'And when I get there?' he asked slowly.

Gaunt was playing with the tuft of hair over his forehead. His expression was mildly surprised – as if the growth were unfamiliar.

'I know your German's fluent. What sort of accent have you got?'

Hendry grinned, happier on familiar territory.

'I speak Hoch Deutsche – let's say the equivalent of your English. Germans assume that I won't blow my nose on my fingers – stuff like that. Don't worry about my accent.'

If Gaunt recognized the sarcasm, he showed no sign of it.

'Good. You can fix your own hotel. As soon as you've booked in, go to 118a Karl Mueller Strasse. You'll be expected. It's the top floor flat– the name's on the door – Schulze.'

Hendry nodded. 'Fair enough. And if anything goes wrong? Don't ask me what – I'm groping.'

Gaunt thumbed a disc of peppermint from the top of the roll – set it where it bulged under his lip.

'That question doesn't arise. Nothing will go wrong.' He crossed the room to stand over Hendry. He reached inside the Canadian's jacket, turning back the tailor's label. He shook his head.

'This is the sort of thing you've got to avoid. Get rid of the clothes you're wearing. You're spending tonight at the

37

Balmoral Hotel, South Kensington. I've had a bag left there with a complete outfit. Carry nothing in your pockets that couldn't belong to Hendrik the journalist. Is that quite clear?'

The implication of inefficiency irritated Hendry. He had to refute it. 'I wore this suit at my trial. My identity wasn't in question.'

'It still isn't,' Gaunt said shortly. 'You're Hendrik the journalist.' He looked at his watch then pressed the bell on the wall. Almost immediately the key was turned in the lock outside. Nobody came into the room.

There was a sense of anti-climax. Hendry came to his feet. 'Is that it – do I go?'

Gaunt jumped from his perch. He stood looking down at the street, his expression hidden. 'It's just occurred to me – we must have joined the army about the same time. In one sense you made a better job of it than I did. I can't help wondering how you managed to find your country's interests more important than your own for five whole years.'

Hendry hesitated. Once again he had the feeling that in some way he was being tested. He tapped his right ear with a finger. 'I've got a hunch you already know. It was the bagpipes – only now I don't hear them any more.'

Gaunt swung round. His smile dissipated the sudden tension. 'You mean you hear but you don't listen. *Auf wiedersehen.*' The German was clumsy.

Big Ben was striking noon as Hendry turned out of Petty France. The cover of the new passport was stiff against his breastbone. Gaunt's forecast of events had been accurate. There had been a long queue of people needing passports in an emergency. His application had been dealt with immediately.

Ever since he had left the hospital he'd known he was tailed. First it had been the man who passed him on the stairs leading up to the photographer – nondescript in overalls, a carpenter's rule sticking out of his pocket. Half an hour later, Hendry slipped into the Post Office on the corner of Trafalgar Square. He was dialling the Flaxman number when he saw the carpenter standing in the queue at the stamp counter. Hendry put the receiver back on its stand. Gaunt's interest in Bernadette was certain. The phone was probably tapped. He left the Post Office without hurrying. Once on the street, he took the steps leading to the subway. The tiled tunnel ahead traversed the square. The sound of running feet echoed behind him. Round the first bend, he stopped. As he started back in the direction he'd come from, the carpenter appeared, trotting with a high exaggerated action. They passed, Hendry's brief nod less bravado than an acceptance of the inevitable. The carpenter stayed with him as far as the Passport Office. The handover to the redfaced clergyman sitting at one of the tables was smooth and unobtrusive. There was no longer any pretence of concealment on either side. When Hendry left the building, the cleric followed sedately, a copy of the *Methodist Times* tucked under his arm. Hendry ducked into the gloom of an Underground station and bought a ticket. Gaunt's attitude went beyond reason. It looked as if they'd throw him back in jail if he saw Bernadette. But if he didn't, he might as well be there.

A westbound train rattled in. The clergyman sat across the aisle, hiding his face behind his newspaper. Hendry leaned back against the lurch of the train, eyes shut. Obviously Gaunt wanted to be sure that he checked in at the Balmoral – what happened after was anyone's guess. It was dangerous underestimating Gaunt. In all probability there'd be a watch on two places. The hotel and Bernadette's house. Yet somehow he had to slip surveillance between now and tonight.

The train rumbled into South Kensington station. The newspaper across the way lowered slightly. For a second the two men stared at one another impassively. Hendry stepped from the coach. As he led the way up Queen's Gate, the clergyman was twenty yards behind.

The front of the Balmoral Hotel was a dingy yellow. Tubbed hydrangeas flanked the steps to the entrance, its blooms faded and dying. He pushed the glass door. A couple of blue-haired matrons sat on the left of the lounge, reading the obituaries. They considered his progress to the deserted reception desk with the frank hostility of permanent residents. He banged the bell half-heartedly. A tired-looking woman with sallow skin bustled out from an inner office. A mirror beside the key rack reflected the street. The clergyman passed the hotel entrance without looking up.

Hendry smiled carefully, aware of the need to make a favourable impression. From here to Cromwell Road, there were two hundred places like this – genteel havens for middle-aged women and retired tea-planters living on pensions. There'd be bridge in the afternoon, a steady consumption of weak gin-and-tonic and the inevitable military wag. He'd expected Gaunt's choice of hotel to be different.

He opened the new passport, displaying the name.

'I believe you've got a room for me.'

The receptionist turned the hotel register with ink-bleared fingers.

'That's right, Mr Hendrik. It's for one night, isn't it? Your bag is up in your room.'

She gave a cursory look at the address he scrawled and thumped the bell firmly. A porter came through the passdoor, wiping his mouth. The women across the lounge watched Hendry's passage to the ancient elevator with speculation.

The bedroom was vast and Victorian. Net curtains draped the windows overlooking the hotel front. The back of the bath-room door was hung with a variety of admonishments. The taps dripped. A scarred leather bag was on the stand against the wall. He lifted the top. There was a smell of mothballs. He spread the clothes on the bed. The brand names and tailors' labels on shirts, suit and underclothing were continental. He slipped on the crêpe-soled shoes, appreciative of Gaunt's eye for detail. Next he tore all identifying marks from his own attire and dumped the garments in the laundry bag. There was an envelope in the jacket he had just donned. He broke the seal. Though the typewritten note was unsigned, the peremptory style was familiar.

Stay in your hotel.

He shredded the piece of paper and flushed the bits down the lavatory bowl. It was going to take more than this to keep him away from the house on Chivers Street. The view from the bedroom windows was unpromising. Immediately underneath, spiked railings protected a basement area from the street.

Neon letters, three feet high, spelled the word Balmoral across the front of the hotel. Once night fell, every window facing the street would be visible from the outside. He opened the bedroom door, a crack at a time. The smell of cooking, the clatter of crockery, drifted up from a lower floor. Across the landing, a stairway wound round the elevator shaft. He closed his door and tiptoed down the steps. A window between floors overlooked a courtyard a dozen feet below. Garbage bins were stacked before the kitchen entrance. Beyond them, a back door gave access to a side street. He tried the window catch. Screws sunk in the framework prevented the sash from lifting. He'd have to find something to deal with them.

He made his way downstairs. As he crossed the empty lounge, he had the impression that something moved behind the reception desk. Without turning his head he knew it was the door to the inner office. He lunched in the small dining-room, eating his way stolidly through the uninspired menu. He left with a table-knife in his pocket. He knew he was still being watched. For the rest of the day he moved from one public room to another, careful to remain on show.

It was nine o'clock when he finished his coffee. He walked across to the desk. The same girl was on duty, the hollows under her eyes stained with fatigue. She managed a smile as he asked for his key.

'You're early, Mr Hendrik.'

He blocked a yawn with his hand. The office door was open. Perched on top of a typewriter was a black, clerical hat. He answered pleasantly.

'That's right. I've an eight o'clock plane to catch. I doubt if there'll be any calls for me but if there are, don't put them through. Would half past six in the morning be too early for tea and orange juice?'

She scribbled on a pad. 'Not at all, Mr Hendrik. Would you like me to make out your bill now?'

The office door was shutting an inch at a time. Hendry nodded. 'You do that.'

He climbed the stairs slowly, managing not to look back. He lay on his bed in the darkness for half an hour, wondering

41

what would happen if he walked straight out of the front doors. Imagination took him no further than a cell.

He swung his legs to the ground and sat listening to the elevator clank to the top floor. As it came to a halt, he slipped out to the landing. He locked the room behind him, gumming a strip of tape from the bottom of the door to the jamb. A few steps took him to the window. He used the table-knife on the screws, snapping the blade twice before they were loose. He climbed on the ledge, shutting the window after him. Then he dropped to the yard. His fall rattled the garbage cans. Through the dirty kitchen windows, the backs of three men showed at the sinks. He ducked low and ran to the yard door. Another second and he was on the street.

The wind had veered to the north, clearing the cloud from an endless sky. The mews cut back to Queen's Gate. A hundred yards away lights flooded the yellow front of the hotel. With any luck, the reverend gentleman in the office would still be looking at his hat. There he'd stay till his relief took over.

A cab dropped Hendry at the bottom of Tite Street. He turned his coat collar up to his ears, walking as a man does on his way home. As he passed the entrance to the cul de sac, he glanced left. Cars were parked on each side of the narrow street, encroaching on the pavements. The centre of the watch on Bernadette's house could be in any one of them.

The coach lantern hanging above her front door was lit. He turned into the next intersection and stopped in the shadow between street lamps. Putting a foot up on the stone coping, he faked a loose shoelace. There was no one in sight.

He vaulted over the low wall and groped his way past the clumsy garden statuary. The sculptor's studio in front of him was unoccupied at night. He felt along the fence to the side gate. It gave under the pressure of his hand.

This route had never failed him. Now no more than a double course of bricks separated him from the little courtyard. He bent his knees, giving his spring an impetus that carried him to the top of the wall. His feet made no sound on the flagged paving as he landed. Something sidled against his legs. He bent down, the black and tan cat arching under his fingers.

This door facing him led to as much of a home as he had known in twenty years. His stupidity had come as near to wrecking it as if he'd driven a bulldozer slap through its middle.

He stepped into the familiar warmth of the kitchen. A pair of nylons floated from the line stretched over the stove. The shopping slate was covered with Bernadette's scrawl. He crossed the room quietly. The glass street door at the end of the darkened passage was a yellow oblong. He felt his way along the wall to the sitting-room. He turned the handle gently, finding the light switch with his free hand.

'Whatever you do, don't raise your voice – they're watching the place from the outside.'

Her face was frightened in the firelight. She was kneeling on the sofa, wearing slacks and a mohair sweater. She covered her mouth with a hand. He took three quick steps, pressed his cheek against hers.

'It's all right, I tell you, darling. I promise you it's all right,' he whispered.

She struggled free. Shaking her head dumbly, she backed to the window. She closed the last chink in the tweed curtains, her eyes apprehensive.

'For God's sake, Kit – what made you come here?'

He kept his voice low, trying to reassure her.

'It's not what you think – they let me out this morning. Your phone's probably tapped – that's why I didn't call you.'

She looked from the instrument to his clothes and back again. 'Tapped?' she repeated unsteadily. 'You shouldn't have come here, Kit. It isn't that I won't help you but you shouldn't have come. What happens if the police find you here?'

She still thought he had broken jail. He threw wood on the fire and helped himself to a drink. 'It isn't the police we've got to worry about, Bernadette.'

She curled up on the sofa, tousle-headed and anxious. In the play of the firelight her face was copper. 'Then who's watching?'

He carried his glass over and sat down beside her. 'Listen to me. Sometimes the truth goes haywire on you – that's what's

43

happened to me. I can't give you any of the answers you need. All I can do is ask you to trust me. I'm free – that's what matters, Bernadette.'

She caught his wrist deliberately. Taking his glass, she set it on the floor.

'What matters is that I love you, Kit! That's basic. It means that I'm sitting here, terrified, wondering what's going to happen to you. I want to help. But surely you see that if I'm going to be any use, I've got to know what I'm doing?'

He looked at her steadily. 'I left that jail through the gate – not over the wall. Tomorrow morning I'm flying to Germany. I need just one break there, darling. That'll give us enough money to forget London and these last two years. I want you to come with me – to marry me.'

She cupped her face in strong slim fingers. She was still wearing the square-cut topaz he had given her. She twisted it nervously. Then she shook her head and looked up.

'You don't just walk out of jail, Kit.'

It was a plea rather than an accusation and somehow it shamed him.

'No,' he said slowly, 'I guess you don't.'

She leaned towards him. 'I said I loved you,' she insisted. 'No matter what you believed all those miserable months it was always true. Loyalty's the big word in your book, Kit. Don't you ever stop to think that I have a right to it?'

He stared at her sombrely. She hit hard and where it hurt. A loyalty that excluded her had no real validity.

'No – I never stopped to think – maybe you're right.'

She reached out, dragging his head down on her breasts. Gradually he relaxed under the play of her hands on the muscles at the top of his shoulders. He went back over the past few days, telling her what he knew without reserve. By the time he was done, the charred log in the grate no longer heated the room. There had been no interruption – no question asked. Now the silence was oppressive.

He disentangled himself from her arms. 'Could be I'm wrong about too many things. With a dozen years jail in front of you there *is* no choice. It's different for you. If you're scared,

I'll understand.' He felt himself on the edge of a pit he had dug with premeditation.

Her quick warm smile rescued him. 'Now you're being foolish. As long as you need me, I'm here.'

This was an echo from long ago – from a windswept beach where gulls swooped under a savage sky. They'd been in trouble then and she had used the same words. The way back to their first understanding might be tough but at least he could see it. His promise was impulsive.

'It's going to be different this time, Bernadette.'

The fire collapsed in ashes. He caught her close as a car door slammed on the street outside. The voices were loud. They sat close, listening as the car backed away. She pulled him up, pushing him along the passage to the kitchen. She closed the door, standing with her back to it.

'It's getting late,' she urged. 'They might miss you. Tell me what you want me to do.'

He checked his watch. He had been in the house too long. He chalked a name on the kitchen slate, gave it to her.

'The Breidenbacher Hof. It's a hotel in Dusseldorf. I'll book a room there for you. Keep away from the phone. Use one of the big agencies for your flight. Make it the day after tomorrow. I'll leave a message at the hotel with my phone number. As soon as you get in, call me. And whatever you do – wherever you go – before you leave, play it as though you were being watched. The chances are you'll be right.'

She sat at the table, the slate in front of her. Her falling hair hid the expression in her eyes.

'There's something I don't get – this man – why couldn't you tell him you wanted me to go to Germany with you? It's what any woman would do in my place – where's the danger in it?'

He answered impatiently. 'I can't even guess. These people think with their heads not their hearts.'

The pulse was large in her throat. She nodded as though his answer satisfied her. 'That letter I wrote – I wouldn't have let you stay in jail to rot, Kit. That's what I was trying to say.

You know that, don't you? I'd have got you out if it had meant climbing the wall myself.'

The seriousness of her face touched him to quick affection. He grinned.

'Sure I know it. Not only because you say so.'

Her smile was back, her dark eyes contented.

'There's one last thing before you go – the lease here – the furniture? I can't just shut the door on it all.'

He touched her hair then bent his mouth to her throat. He refused to say the word goodbye. 'Hire an agent to handle it. All you have to worry about is being on that plane. I'll see you, darling, and take care.' He lifted a hand and stepped through the kitchen door to the tiny garden.

He gained the hotel yard unnoticed. Through the windows tired voices were still bawling at one another. Darkness covered him as he clambered on top of a garbage can. He took a good grip on the ledge overhead and hauled himself up. For some reason or other the window resisted his pressure. He used the heels of his hands, sitting right down into the sill in an effort to budge the framework. It was useless. The catch was undone but the screws on the inside had been replaced. He dropped back to the yard, crouching as he considered his next move. The locked escape route obliged him to use the front entrance. The replacement of the screws was unlikely to be coincidental. His early-to-bed routine had probably fooled no one. The only thing left was to bluff it out. He could admit leaving the hotel without mentioning Chivers Street. It was certain that nobody had seen him leave or enter the house.

He didn't know how he'd explain climbing from the back window. Time enough when they challenged him.

He closed the yard door and circled the block. The front entrance was open. As he crossed the lounge, the last stragglers from the television room were yawning their way out. The office behind the desk was shut tight. The busy night porter paid him no heed.

Once out of sight, the Canadian took the stairs at the trot. Outside his bedroom door, he felt for the piece of cellulose tape. It lay on the floor where it had been pulled away. He switched on the light. Nothing appeared to have been disturbed. He undressed hurriedly and pulled the blankets over his head. Sleep was a dark pool. Gradually he sank beneath its surface.

6

GAUNT LET himself into the quiet house. The Chief's overcoat draped the front of the grandfather's clock. His shabby hat hung on its accustomed hook. Gaunt pushed the soundproof door of the study. The top half of the Chief's vast body was wedged in a chair. A footstool carried the weight of his legs. He opened his eyes as Gaunt dropped the suitcase on the floor.

The question was prompt. 'Well?'

Gaunt's face was rueful. 'You must have a nose for this sort of thing, sir. He followed your line – not mine. Out one of the back windows in his hotel – then a lot of acrobatics and into the woman's house. He stayed there for nearly three hours.'

The Chief lifted his head, disturbing nothing lower than his neck. His expression was mildly satisfied.

'You can't ignore the emotional factor, George. To use a term that always bothers you, the man's in love. The obvious thing was to put him on a plane straight from jail.'

There was no criticism that was not shared yet Gaunt moved restlessly.

'I'd have sworn I had him bottled up for the night – that's the impression he gave me this morning. He's either more stupid than I thought or I am.'

The Chief put his feet down. 'It's the same old story – pressure of time. We're being hurried into snap judgements and that's bad. We've allowed him to be more or less mobile. He can tell this woman what he wants on a postcard, surely. I don't follow your objection to him seeing her.'

Gaunt bathed his hands in the warm air from the space

heater. He was being asked to justify his decision, not explain it.

'If it weren't for the man Proctor, there wouldn't *be* any objection. You've read the report, sir. Proctor's been the woman's lover for two years. He was in her house tonight. In fact he left half an hour before Hendry climbed over the back wall.'

The Chief searched a drawer for a pipe. He rammed coarse-cut tobacco into the bowl and spoke from an acrid cloud.

'And if he hadn't left?'

Gaunt gave the thought the reflection it merited.

'Hendry's no good to us on a charge of murder. That's what it'll come to if he's ever sure of his facts. And make no mistake, if she goes to Germany, she'll take Proctor with her.'

The Chief sucked judiciously.

'Why *should* she go – she's got what she wants here, hasn't she?'

Gaunt leaned forward, emphasizing his own certainty.

'There's something else she needs – money. And that's precisely what Hendry represents to her. You may be the expert on women, sir, but I know what makes this one tick.'

He reached across the desk for the red scramble-phone and handed the spare receiver to his senior. He dialled a number. An American voice answered his call.

'George – sorry I had to keep you waiting. Here's what we've got on your inquiry. She was born Bernadette Clouder in Tulsa, Oklahoma, 1921. The father's described as a steel erector. From the name, I'd say the mother was off a Cherokee Reservation. There's an uninvolved history of High School and College – then a couple of years in Phoenix, Arizona, working as secretary. She got her passport in New York eleven years ago. It's valid for all countries this side of the Curtain. There's no FBI record and this is the first time she's come to our attention. We don't have a thing on her – who's she killed?'

Gaunt smiled thinly at the man across the desk.

'Nobody. It's the wrong woman, Harry – the background doesn't match.'

The man's voice was affable but tired. 'Liar. Well, the sun never sets and all that. Up here on Grosvenor Square we sleep. Good night.'

Gaunt put the receiver on the stand. 'Well, that's that. I can fill in the rest myself. She's been in and out of the country for the past seven years – always reported to the Alien's Office. We daren't take a chance holding her. She'd shout her head off.'

The elder man sank lower into his chair. He picked interestedly at his water-logged pipe.

'I can let you know when and if she leaves the country. Without her to worry about I'd have said you were home and dried. What time do you get to Dusseldorf?'

'Two in the morning. The forecast is rain and sleet from the Rhine to the Baltic. I'll never understand why I didn't stay in a nice draughty barrack in Aldershot.'

The Chief's chin dropped nearer his chest.

'Bryant's called a meeting for Tuesday night. I'll expect news before then. Whatever happens, you'll be in the clear, George. And look after yourself.'

Gaunt picked up his bag. Only physical displacement could relieve the growing sense of urgency.

'I'll do that, sir. There's one thing I haven't told you. Some bloody fool shut the window after Hendry tonight. He'll know he's being watched. All I can do now is not let him forget it.'

7

SHE WOKE to the sound of a plane droning overhead and flicked the switch on the bedside table. She turned the lamp away, shading her eyes. The bedroom was in unaccustomed disorder. Stockings and underwear trailed from open drawers – a jumble of coats sagged on the back of a chair. In front of the cupboard was the bag she had packed the moment Hendry had left. She rolled on her side, remembering the narrowness of her escape – the open street door, Proctor's face under the lamp as they'd said good night. It seemed only minutes afterwards that the light had gone out in the sitting-room. Then there was Hendry, whispering from the doorway. Those first seconds, she could think of nothing but Proctor's pyjamas hanging on the bathroom door – his razor on top of the medicine chest. Once Hendry was gone, her first impulse had been to run. She crammed clothes into a case with desperate haste, starting at every sound in the silent house. As though he'd be back at any minute, done with pretence and ready to kill her. She'd sat irresolute, long after midnight. Gradually reason replaced fear.

The black-faced clock on her dresser buzzed hidden alarm, skeetering sideways across the glass top. She kicked back the bedclothes and ran to silence it. By the time she had finished her bath, the morning exodus outside had begun. She stood behind the curtain, drying the last damp spot between her breasts and watching the street. The doctor's Ford was there – the insurance broker's Jaguar – the jalopy loaded with empty wine bottles. It was the usual nine o'clock scene. There were no lounging strangers, no sinister vehicles. Funny the way Kit's fantasies were always bolstered with theatrical detail. She dressed and went downstairs, collecting the morning papers on her way to the kitchen. She ate a sketchy breakfast, searching the newspapers from cover to cover. The item she expected to find was not there.

She drew the sitting-room curtains and used the phone without a second thought. The showdown with Proctor's mother could no longer be delayed.

'I'd like to speak to Philip, if you please.'

Mrs Proctor's mannered voice was adamant.

'I'm afraid my son isn't available. Who shall I say telephoned?'

She smiled at herself in the mirror. 'Bernadette Jeffries. I don't suppose you know the name but your son spent the night before last in my house. It would save a great deal of unpleasantness if you got him out of bed.'

The phone went dead. It was only seconds before Proctor came on the line. She cut through his invective impatiently.

'I don't *care*, Philip! Worry about me, not your mother. Something came up – I've got to see you. Be here before ten thirty.' She put the phone down. The mother might be a fool but not the son. He'd be on time.

She stood in front of the mirror, twisting her body so that she could see her stocking seams. Three-inch heels on her shoes accentuated her height. The dull gold turban made a barbaric foil to her black cashmere coat. She closed the street door behind her. The King's Road eccentrics were already abroad – haughtily surveyed through dark glasses by the first patrons of the coffee bars. She turned into the bank entrance, clicking across the floor to the cashier she knew.

'I'm closing the account, Mr Bell. I'll take my balance in cash.'

He smiled without parting his lips. 'I'm sorry about that, Mrs Jeffries. We shall miss you.'

She looked at him steadily. The arch familiarity was of a piece with the milkman's knowing wink, the clucking sympathy of her maid. If anything, the neighbourhood had enjoyed the wide publicity given to Kit's conviction.

'I'm sure you will,' she said shortly. 'Now if you don't mind, I'm in a hurry.'

She'd been back at the house minutes when she heard the cab arrive outside. She ran to the sitting-room window. Proctor wore neither hat nor overcoat. Thin mouth set, he shoved change into the driver's hand and hurried to the front door. She let him in. He stood in the hall, looking at her without speaking. Then without change of expression he whipped the flat of his hand across her cheeks. Her head rocked with the force of the blows. She started to retreat into the sitting-room. He came after her. Finally the wall prevented her from going farther.

Anger dragged his face to ugliness. 'You rotten bitch! Why did you have to do it? Do you realize what you've done? I'm out – chucked out!'

She slipped by him cautiously and hid the pain of her face over the bubbling percolator. She filled a cup and gave it to him.

'Drink this coffee – you'll feel better.'

A flush climbed above his collar. He swung his arm violently, sending the cup to crash against the wall. A brown stain spread on the carpet. She filled a second cup and put it on the little table by his side. This was the first time he had ever struck her. She was curious at the lack of resentment. It was as if this was what she had been waiting for.

'You don't have to go back,' she said quietly. 'From now on your home's with me. Please drink your coffee.'

He lowered himself heavily into the chair. He stared at the cup by his side. For a split second it seemed that he was about to send it after the first. Suddenly he dragged his tie from his neck, unbuttoning his collar. His voice was menacing.

'You're going to pick up that phone and tell my mother you lied to her. I don't care if you have to grovel – but tell her you lied.'

She was standing at the tall glass, dabbing the smeared mascara from the corners of her eyes. The red weals still flared on her cheeks. She kept her back to him.

'Kit's out. He came here last night just after you left.' In the glass she watched his body stiffen then relax.

He came to his feet lazily. Putting both hands on her shoulders he forced her round so that his face was no more than inches from hers. He let her go with a sudden sound of disgust.

'You must take me for a halfwit, Bernadette. I'll give you thirty seconds to make the call.'

She answered doggedly. 'I'm telling you Kit was in this room last night.'

He snatched the morning paper from the desk. She shook her head.

'You won't find anything there. He hasn't broken jail. He was released yesterday morning.'

His heavy jaw hardened. 'Not through the gate, he wasn't. If he's out, he's done it the hard way. In that case I can understand your concern. In your place I'd be in Australia by now or at least Iceland.'

She let him get halfway to the hall before she replied. 'And leave thirty thousand pounds behind?'

He turned on his heel, his pale eyes widening. 'What is that supposed to mean?' he asked cautiously.

She walked across to the phone. Her voice was casual as she lifted the handset.

'What exactly do you want me to say to your mother?'

He caught her wrist, smiling. 'I'm sorry, darling. I do it again and again and I never learn. Tell me what happened.'

He heard her out, his head tipped back and his eyes blank. It was the pose of a man reluctantly prepared to suspend disbelief. Finally he answered her.

'Where do you see thirty thousand pounds in that?'

She frowned, refusing to accept the implication. 'I know how Kit's mind works. He tells nobody what he does, least of all me. Not until he's sure that he's got what he's after. This cloak-and-dagger business isn't meant to convince me. He doesn't even care whether I believe it! But he had to produce some sort of story that would cover the facts. Don't you see that? I've never thought that the Benurian securities *were* destroyed. Now I'm sure of it. They're still in Germany and that's why Kit's gone there.'

He dropped his cigarette in the cup at his feet. 'I understand facts. A week ago Hendry went inside for twelve years. We know he hasn't appealed. Suddenly here he is climbing over your back wall. I'm waiting for someone to tell me how.'

She was losing her patience. 'Does it matter how – he's out, isn't he? I don't believe in miracles any more than you do. I called the Lufthansa desk at London Airport at a quarter to nine this morning. Someone named Christopher Hendrik was on the Dusseldorf flight. Check it yourself. Who knows how he's done it! For all we know maybe he bribed his way out.'

He made a pile of the broken crockery, stretching out the tip of a black polished brogue. 'Bribed who? The Prison Commissioners, for instance? This is England, Bernadette.'

Her voice broke angrily. Instead of planning, they were sitting here wrangling.

'Then you do better. Suppose you provide the answer!

Would you rather have Kit's story. Agents, hospitals – a safe in the middle of nowhere?'

He ran the knot of his tie up to his throat. 'No – I don't like that either. It's as dotty as your theory. No government organization needs to go recruiting in the Old Bailey. They have qualified men of their own and no headaches afterwards.'

Her resentment was explosive. Nothing she said was getting by this wall of obstinacy.

'So what *do* you think – nothing? The one time in my life when I know what I'm doing and you sit there sniping at me. Why is it that women always have to make your decisions for you, Philip?'

He leaned back, scratching himself luxuriously. 'But you're wrong – they don't. It's an illusion you all have.'

The smugness stung her to indiscretion. 'Illusions! Well, don't think I have any left about you! The gentleman-adventurer production may go down well with Chelsea art students but I know the real McCoy. He needs a skirt for a shelter.'

He seemed completely indifferent to the insult in her voice. His smile broadened.

'And Hendry didn't? Is that what you mean? I can never understand why you went to so much trouble to get rid of him.'

Her throat tightened with shock. She wet her lips, making a frantic attempt to meet his look. She managed no more than a dull repetition of the accusation.

'Get rid of him?'

He locked both hands behind his neck, obviously enjoying himself. 'What in the world would I do without you? Have you spent all these weeks imagining I didn't know who put Hendry inside?'

She gripped her hands together so tight that it was painful.

'No. No, you're wrong, Philip.'

'But I'm *right*, Bernadette,' he mocked. 'You knew Pell had the needle to him. You had a key to Hendry's cottage. You had another one cut. I saw you hand it over. You were wearing the same hat and coat you've got on now. You took a seventy-four bus along the Cromwell Road and met Pell in the entrance of the Victoria and Albert Museum. They pinched Hendry the next day.'

'Give me a cigarette,' she said suddenly. She watched his face as he struck a match, looking for some sign of sympathy. There was none.

'Just how long have you been spying on me?' she asked bitterly.

He waved a casual, deprecating hand. 'I like to know exactly what I'm getting into. You see, I've always respected your determination.'

Tears gathered disregarded in her eyes. She had no idea why she was crying except that everything he said was unfair. For two years she'd lived on the back of a lie, defending their happiness. Philip had neither helped nor discouraged her. He'd been content to freewheel just as long as the money lasted. He'd always been relaxed and detached, unconcerned that she was getting nowhere in her attempt to force a break with Kit.

Finally something more than desperation had sent her to Pell. The detective-inspector had made it all sound so easy – even reasonable. She had every right to free herself from a man for whom she felt nothing but fear – a man who belonged behind bars anyway.

'What I did was for you,' she said slowly.

'For yourself,' he corrected. 'It's about time you and I took the gloves off, Bernadette. You're looking for the impossible – a man you can dominate as well as respect. Hendry carried too many guns for you but you still use him as a yardstick to hit me over the head. He never lived on women – the big successful crook. In fact, he seems to have had all the right attitudes. But there was still something you couldn't get your hooks into. With me you thought it would be different.'

She drove herself to resist the smooth gibing voice.

'Your charm's getting a little chipped round the edges, Philip. I'm not so sure that I need it. Kit's waiting for me – I can be in Germany in a couple of hours.'

He rose to his feet, brushing ash from the soft blue stuff of his jacket. He smiled like someone who hears a familiar but well-liked story.

'Don't be stupid. You're not going anywhere without me, Bernadette. You and my mother have the same idea — but you're both wrong. I never was for sale. And I'm a lot smarter than Hendry. I've been to jail once. I don't intend letting it happen again.'

'It never will,' she promised. 'Not as long as you have me on your side.'

He was still showing his good strong teeth. 'I'm delighted to hear it. You're as unscrupulous as I am. It helps. What about cash — this trip's going to cost money?'

On her feet she was as tall as he was. Nothing mattered, she thought, as long as he was coming to Germany with her. She was ultra-careful in victory. 'I've already been to the bank. I closed out the account.'

He was in front of the mirror, frowning at the bald spot on the crown of his head. He turned slowly. She opened her handbag and counted out a hundred pounds.

'There's a plane for Dusseldorf at twelve thirty tomorrow morning. We'll go on that. You'd better book your own seat.'

He put the notes away in a sealskin wallet. She put a hand on his arm. Money always seemed to mellow him. There must be some half-forgotten spot — Central America, maybe — where Kit would never follow. Sun and sea would burn the puffiness from Philip's body. She wanted him to understand how she felt.

'Would you rather I collected your things from your mother's place? It might not be so pleasant for you.'

He shook his head. 'I've been waiting for this for thirty-eight years. I wouldn't miss it.'

She went as far as the hall with him. 'You'll be back later?'

He stood in the open doorway. 'Just as soon as I've packed my bags,' he assured her.

8

THE EASTBOUND cabs were all occupied. He walked along the King's Road in the direction of Sloane Square. The Saturday morning monkey parade spilled from supermarket to vegetable store, milling on the pavements in front of the coffee bars. The street had changed in the twenty years he had known it, not the characters. They still hurried from North Country Polytechnics, Berkshire finishing schools, the Universities, to strike the blow for freedom.

Resting actors, young men of letters despising the writer who made a living at his craft, the art students lofty with ideals and with stolen paint brushes in their jeans. As long as your ideals were lofty you were in. The young and well-to-do married couples were an effective solvent. Whether these people escaped from studio, bed-sitter or Sloane Avenue *bijou residence*, the same troubled spirit seemed to drive them. As if for a couple of hours a week the street offered mystery, romance and above all reassurance in one economy-size package. One in a hundred made the grade, conformity reclaimed most of the others. The worst end of all lay somewhere between the two extremes. Too easily it could have been his own.

The Chelsea layabout, running out of years and hair. Living on eggs fried over a gas ring – rent paid monthly in advance, no washing hung in the rooms and no lady visitors. The old school tie was always frayed at the knot, the voice at your elbow from the World's End to the Square.

Good God if it isn't Jeremy! Well no, I haven't. Actually I've been in the Bahamas.

Bernadette's remark about thinning charm was a bit near the knuckle. Only the fivers in his wallet softened the impact. He had to be doubly careful with her now. What she called her love for him had to be encouraged. The image, as they say, preserved. Violence she'd accept only if it was the framework

57

of affection. There could be no more slapped faces, no more coffee cups chucked at the wall. Sweetness and light on the other hand would only put her on her guard. He had to find the compromise between what he was and what she thought he was.

A youngster with a collar of dandruff blocked Proctor's way. He was trilling some genteel piece of affectation into a parked E type Jaguar. Proctor trod firmly on the splayed flying boot. The sudden alarm in the young man's face pleased him.

'Over and out *and* Roger,' Proctor said happily. He was still in good humour when the cab reached Fleet Street. The tavern was crowded. He shouldered through reporters on temporary leave of absence from the neighbouring news rooms. The fat barman was sweating at his beer engine. He filled one tankard after another with harassed dexterity. A long, steady pull on the handle – a couple of flicks to put a head on the brew and he added a glass to the line on the wet bar. He dispensed his beer to the first hand he saw holding a coin in his direction. A layer of tobacco smoke hung under the beamed ceiling, blurring the lights. Everyone talked and nobody listened.

The bartender rested his arm for a moment. Proctor leaned across the counter.

'Tell Jerry Nolan I'd like a word with him. I'll be over in the corner.'

The two-shilling piece vanished into the fat man's apron pocket. He moved away to the far end of the bar. Proctor carried his glass to a table against the wall. For no apparent reason, there was breathing space here. He sat under a haphazard array of press photographs, watching Nolan come across the room.

The reporter set his drink on the table. His thick short hair looked as if it had been cut by a lawn mower. He spoke through his flattened nose rather than his mouth.

'What ill wind blew you in here?'

Proctor hooked a toe under the rung of a chair. He kicked the seat at Nolan, smiling carefully:

'One of these days when you're not looking, Jerry, I'm going to punch you right between the eyes.'

Nolan wiped spilled beer from the chair, using the bottom of his trench coat. He lowered himself ungraciously.

'The only time I see you is when you need something. The last time it cost me a tenner. That was a year ago. Some snide little yarn about a fine you had to pay. Like a fool, I went for it.'

Proctor reached inside his jacket. He eased a couple of five pound notes from the loaded wallet, making sure that Nolan glimpsed the reserve.

'There's your tenner, Jerry. For another twenty I need some information.'

Nolan drew his hand back leaving the money untouched. 'Ah no! We've been through this before. There's nothing do-ing.'

Proctor put the wallet away. He swivelled his back to the bar, his voice for Nolan alone.

'Stop acting like somebody's grandmother. You're a crime reporter. I'm not asking you whose jewellery is where. This is a simple inquiry – I could handle it myself.'

'Then do that,' Nolan said shortly.

Proctor smiled. 'The Scotch is getting at your memory, old man. I could have had you out of a job any time over the last three years. Listening to your hubble-bubble put me in prison for six months, remember?'

Nolan wiped a hand across a nervous mouth. 'You asked me to do you a favour.'

'I asked you to give me some information,' Proctor re-proved. 'For twenty-five per cent of what we made.'

'All I did was repeat what I was told.'

Proctor was drawing circles with his finger in the beer. He looked up. 'But you made it sound good, Jerry. Good enough for me to take a chance on. A refugee diamond broker with a fortune in stones hidden under his bed. And every Friday night, the flat's empty while he goes to a synagogue. Only there wasn't any fortune – or any synagogue. Just a bastard ten feet tall who locked me in a cupboard till the police came. You must have had some sort of conscience.' He showed the other

59

man the typewritten sheet of paper. 'The note you sent me when I was on bail.'

Nolan smelled his drink, swallowed it and looked at his shoes. 'Plain paper and written on somebody else's machine.'

Proctor shrugged. 'But your signature. Anyway, we're not going to put it to the test. You know, you're not being intelligent. I'm offering you twenty quid and your note back for something it'll take you a few minutes to find out. A phone call and a glance through your files. That's all you're asked for.'

Nolan's clothes seemed to grow too big for him. His flattened nose and mouth were morose. 'Do me a favour – avoid me in future. What's the inquiry?'

Proctor looked at his watch. It was after noon.

'A man called Christopher Hendry was sentenced to twelve years at the last Old Bailey. I want to know which jail he's in – everything you have on record about a job he pulled five years ago. It was a safe robbery involving securities belonging to an Armenian called Benurian. Find out from your City Editor how easy or hard it would have been to put that stuff on the market. And, Jerry . . .'

Nolan was listening attentively, head down. He raised it. 'What?'

'This time I want fact not fiction.'

The reporter climbed to his feet. 'I'll be back as soon as I can.'

Proctor bought a plate of sandwiches and carried them to his place in the corner. An hour passed before Nolan appeared through the door at the bottom of the stairs. He sat down and pushed a manila envelope across the table.

'It's all there – everything we have in the files. He got away with negotiable securities listed at thirty-two thousand quid. I talked to the City Desk. The stuff would be worth slightly more at today's prices. Getting rid of it is another question. Everyone thinks it's possible but doesn't know how. This much is certain. None of that stock has ever come on the market.'

Proctor took a deep breath. 'What about Hendry?'

Nolan stank of whisky. He looked genuinely puzzled. 'A

blank wall. It's a funny thing. I've tried everyone likely to help. The Prison Commissioners, the Home Office – the Yard. The PRO there owes me a favour. Even he can tell me nothing.'

'So you don't know what jail he's in?' asked Proctor.

'No. I rang his lawyer of record who said Wandsmoor. The Governor there has no comment. It's an odd one but I get the impression he's out and not in.'

Proctor's eyes were shrewd. 'I know he is. Tell me this. In your experience, have you ever heard of anyone bribing his way out of prison in England?'

Nolan blinked. 'I wouldn't put it that way. Let's say being released for services rendered. Yes. Frequently.'

Proctor gave it thought. The truth had to be somewhere between this and Bernadette's theory. The police had framed Hendry. It might have been done to force him into some kind of a deal.

'What could Hendry know that would be so important to the law?' he asked. 'They had their conviction for the securities. The police don't work overtime for insurance companies. What could he have to offer?'

Nolan's face was happy for the first time. 'You're not dealing with a mechanic, Philip. This man's a top-flight operator. Even with us he gets a file under his own name. When a top-flight decides to talk, heads roll. I've an idea I'll be getting a story soon. A good one.'

Proctor opened his wallet. They were both right. Nolan and Bernadette. Hendry's way out was by pulling someone else in.

When it came to thirty thousand pounds, the Canadian was no different from anyone else. Proctor counted twenty pounds. He pushed them into Nolan's hand. 'There you are, Jerry.' He held the typewritten note up again, quoting the byline used by the reporter. '"No one ever gagged him"! You'll write this particular story when I send you back this note and not before.'

His mother's flat was in a house perched on the uppermost slope of Campden Hill. A bleak grey mansion converted to maisonettes for those caring more for a good address than warmth and privacy. The hall and stairway were common property, cluttered with the bric-à-brac of the resident owner – an elderly spinster who glided about the house smiling weakly. As always, the place gave Proctor a feeling of acute depression.

The doors that blocked off each landing were kept tightly shut – the people who lived behind them rarely seen. What neighbourly communication was necessary was conducted either by telephone or notes left on the downstairs hall table.

He let himself into his mother's flat, pausing inside for the inevitable summons. This time it came from the drawing-room. He turned the handle slowly. Her choice of setting was typical. She was being the châtelaine, surrounded by silver frames and regency stripes. She was sitting at her writing desk, the figure of authority. She took off her spectacles as he entered, writing till he reached the exact centre of the room.

'Would you mind closing the door behind you, Philip – there's something I have to say to you.'

She carried her weight and age with assurance. The white hair was tinged with lavender and carefully groomed, her mouth discreetly outlined with lipstick.

He ignored her request. He walked to the single bar heater she permitted and warmed his legs. They lived completely alone but for the housekeeper's daily visit. Yet his mother still conducted her interviews as though servants listened behind each door.

'I thought we had your final word this morning,' he remarked casually.

She spoke with a sort of religious puritanism.

'I'm still waiting for an explanation of your disgraceful behaviour, Philip.'

He laughed at her. 'You're making yourself ridiculous, Mother. I'm leaving – I only came back to pack. You can go on steaming open my letters – I'm sure they'll confirm your worst suspicions.'

She made a sound of exasperation. 'And where do you

propose to go? Don't tell me this woman's fool enough to take you in?'

He spread his legs, remembering every past indignity.

'Why not?' he taunted. 'She probably thinks I'll make a good husband. What do *you* think?'

She moved to the front door with ungainly speed. She locked it from the inside and put the key in her bag. She sat down again, breathing a little heavily.

'You're not leaving this house, Philip. I refuse to be humiliated in this way.'

He raised his shoulders. 'We've played the scene fifty times, Mother. I know exactly what's worrying you. None of your jewellery is missing – you've counted your bits of jade – inspected your cheque-book. Everything's normal – if you can use the expression in this house with a straight face. So how is it that I can leave your bed and board? It's simple – I've had a better offer.'

Her cheeks turned an unhealthy colour.

'How dare you say a thing like that?' she said quietly. 'At least wait until I'm dead before you disgrace me completely.'

His words were ruthless. 'People have always been afraid to tell you the truth, Mother. It's about time I did it. You've been a vicious-tongued, domineering old dragon all your life. Now you're terrified there'll be nobody left for you to bully. Believe me, escape from this rat-race isn't a disgrace.'

She was suddenly an old and haggard woman.

'Don't do it, Philip – don't go. I know that you're safe as long as you stay here.'

He was completely unmoved by her plea.

'It isn't me you're thinking about but yourself. You're an old woman, afraid of being left alone with the mess you've made of your life. You haven't been able to pull the wool over my eyes since Father died. You were glad when I went to prison. It gave you another victim.'

He went into his bedroom, indifferent to her outburst of weeping. He packed methodically, ignoring her as she clawed hysterically at his hands and body. He carried his bags as far as the locked front door. She stood like an aged hound aware of impending disaster. He fastened his overcoat and held out a hand. His voice had no emotion.

'The key, Mother.'

She was trembling violently. 'Don't go, Philip,' she repeated herself – 'You mustn't go.'

His hand stretched over the phone on the hall table.

'If you don't give me that key, I'm going to dial for the police. I shall say I'm being held here against my will.'

She moved as though drugged, replacing the key in the lock but not turning it. She spoke with an effort as if sobered by some icy deluge.

'Living or dead, I never want to see you again.' She went into the drawing-room and closed the door.

He phoned for a cab and carried his bags downstairs. He had no regrets – only a sense of complete freedom. Once in the cab, he was too busy considering the implications of his move to look back at the street. As the car drove off, a man left a doorway opposite, jumped on a motor scooter and followed.

9

A COLD THIN rain was falling at Lohausen Airport. Oil-skinned handlers ran the wheeled steps to the side of the plane. A ground stewardess waited on the glistening tarmac, a white chiffon scarf tied round her saucer-like hat. She herded the disembarking passengers into a railed pen with the skill of a well-trained collie. Metal barriers ahead steered the single file of arrivals past a hatchway with a raised window.

Hendry shuffled forward. He pushed his passport across the ledge and into the ready hand. The man's stubby fingers flipped the pages with practised surety. The blue-and-gold cover gleamed under the strong lamp. Only the top half of the police officer's body was visible. His round grey head and burly shoulders seemed to have no contact with the ground.

'Mr Hendrik?'

Hendry nodded. After a week living on the fringe of reality, he was almost ready to believe in his bogus identification. But this man was trained to detect the nuance as well as the obvious. A shading of ink, a misplaced stamp, a false response or appearance. What looked like a casual and routine inspection could be misleading.

The official smiled. He whacked the passport on the ledge like a man testing a counterfeit coin. His English was faultless.

'Have a good time in Germany.'

The customs formalities were equally harmless. Hendry carried his bag past the expectant group at the gate leading to the main arrival hall. He stood uncertainly by an empty bench, looking into the crowd for a sign of either challenge or welcome. The faces were blank and bored.

He walked across and scanned the names on the envelopes pinned to the bulletin board. Nothing there concerned him.

Outside, he lifted an arm at the first of a line of squat, diesel cabs. The interior of the car was heavy with the scent of freesias. A small vase hung under the dashboard. The driver peered through the arcs of his windscreen wipers. Shoulders hunched, he waited for his directions.

Hendry was staring at the back of the man's neck. There was something familiar about the two thick folds of skin rising above the collar – the expanse of pale blond hair between stubby ears. He tried to fit time and place to the memory.

'Sybelstrasse,' he said finally.

The driver's head jerked impatiently. 'Ja, Sybelstrasse – but which end?'

Hendry's toes curled. It was as though the driver had asked a highly personal question.

'Whichever end you like – it doesn't matter.'

The man wrenched himself round, creaking leather. He flapped a hand at the meter.

'But *there* it matters! Which number Sybelstrasse?'

The tight band around Hendry's nerve centres uncoiled. He

settled back in his seat. He'd never seen the man in his life before.

'Two hundred and sixty.'

Gradually the flat fields surrounding the airport were replaced by high-walled factories. British Army signposts offered code directions to military traffic. The cab turned east at the streetcar tracks. Great articulated trucks on their way to the *autobahn* lurched dangerously near. The tall apartment buildings had an air of permanence. There was an impression of communal discipline – an indifference to the Englishman's need of a patch of green and sagging fence. The driver slowed for the lights at the foot of the Königsallee. The length of the broad, tree-decked street was divided by an ornamental canal. Elegant stores lined its east side. Across the stretch of water were the banks and offices, symbols of the wealth of the *Rührgebiet*. Beyond these a tall slender structure of glass and steel towered over the city. The tempo was North American rather than European. The crowds on the pavement by the lights had the same look of strained dedication to success. After England it was as foreign as sauerkraut.

He dismissed the cab on a quiet street off the Brehmplatz. The small hotel bore no sign or mark to distinguish it from the rest of the stone-built residences. Most of these had been built when Dusseldorf still had a zoo. Now the animals were gone, leaving only the park that gave the district its name. He rang the doorbell. The girl who greeted him spoke in shy primer English. There was little to tell him. She ran the place with the help of a couple of maids. No meals were served after breakfast. She hoped he would be comfortable.

His room was pleasantly warm after the Victorian chilliness of the Balmoral. The window overlooked a garden already gripped by winter. Leaves floated on the slimy surface of a small concrete swimming pool. At the far end of a stretch of sodden grass a wooden gate led to a yard and garage. Beyond these, a driveway connected with a side road. It was a perfect layout for a man who needed to be mobile.

He spread the map of the city across his bed, taking his

bearings. From here on, the fewer questions he had to ask, the better. The address of the rendezvous Gaunt had given him lay off the Grafenberger Allee – at a guess, ten minutes' walk distant. He locked his room and went downstairs. Outside the cold rain had stopped. He walked past washed gardens to Karl Mueller Strasse. The peaceful street was built only on one side. A line of small apartment houses faced a school set in a tiny park. Beyond the shrubs and bushes streetcars rattled along the main thoroughfare. A tree nursery extended behind the three and four-family houses. Hendry walked past windows filled with burgeoning greenery, checking the numbers as he went. 118a was the last house. Plate glass slashed its grey, stone front. Up on the top story, a bright orange canvas cover was lashed to the front of the balcony – a memory of summer. He climbed a short flight of steps to the closed glass door. Down below the railings on his right, a steep ramp rose from the underground garage to the street. There were five name plates – the one he needed was at the top.

SCHULZE, WOLFGANG – VERTRETER

He pressed a bell. A buzzer sounded distantly, releasing the street door. He closed it behind him and started up the stairway. As he neared the third floor, he saw the middle-aged Japanese waiting in the open doorway. The man greeted him, smiling politely. For a moment Hendry floundered – caught unaware by the incongruity of the Asiatic's German.

The Canadian propped himself against the railing.

'Herr Schulze?' Even as he spoke, he realized that he had pressed the wrong bell.

The Japanese shook his head, pointing at the stairs.

'*Oben*,' he said and shut his door.

There was a tiny inspection glass on the top floor. Hendry tried to look beyond it. The bubble-glass allowed only one-way vision. He rapped hard with his knuckles. The summons was answered immediately. Gaunt had discarded his country clothes. His black suit and tie gave him the drab decency of a professional mute. The skin stretched tight across his cheekbones and his eyelids were an angry violet. He spoke impatiently.

'Well, come in, for God's sake – don't stand there like a bailiff.'

He hung Hendry's overcoat on a hanger in the hall – led the way into a room that ran the complete depth of the building. The end walls were mostly window. French doors gave access to balconies front and rear. Beyond Gaunt was a glimpse of a neat bedroom. Bare bookshelves and empty flower vases told the story of a place rarely used. A fit of coughing left Gaunt struggling for breath. He wiped his eyes.

'Asthma – it's this bloody climate.' He grinned like a fox. 'Your chin's hanging on your chest, man. What did you expect – false beards?'

Hendry shrugged. The initial surprise of seeing Gaunt was over. He watched the Englishman cautiously, wondering just how much Gaunt knew of the visit to Bernadette.

'We've had everything else.'

Gaunt fished a key from his trouser pocket. He snapped it on a metal ring, laid it on the arm of Hendry's chair.

'Whenever you come here in future, use this. It fits both doors – the one downstairs and the one on the landing. Where are you staying?'

Hendry gave the name of his hotel. He was spinning the key round his forefinger, his expression thoughtful.

'That note you left for me last night – I thought of asking the clergyman up to the room – we could have held evening prayers.'

Gaunt turned away. He dragged the curtains in front of the far window, putting that half of the room in darkness. He showed no sign that he had heard.

Hendry lolled over the side of his chair. He trailed the key-ring across the carpet, following the line of the pattern. There was an outside chance that an hotel employee had replaced the screws – an inquisitive maid broken the seal on his door. He had to know the truth.

'If you'd been there, we might even have sung a couple of hymns,' he persisted. 'I went for a walk instead – a long walk.'

Gaunt's comment was brief. 'I know what you did.'

He carried a screen and movie projector from the bedroom. Kneeling on the floor, he assembled them in silence. When the screen was taut on its frame, he came to his feet like a cow, rear end first. He brushed the dirt from his trousers. The upper part of his body was in shadow.

'How long ago is it since you saw Philip Proctor?' he asked casually.

Hendry stiffened, searching his memory in vain. He sensed a trap that was camouflaged. Suddenly he had the answer. He wasn't suspected of leaving the hotel to see Bernadette but a man he'd never heard of. Somehow, Gaunt's signals were crossed. Hendry dropped his false nonchalance.

'Who the hell's Philip Proctor?'

Gaunt moved behind the projector, making adjustments to the lens.

'Nobody in particular – I just thought he might have been a chum of yours.'

'I don't have chums,' Hendry said shortly. 'I'm in the wrong business.'

Gaunt seemed content to take the discussion no further. He made Hendry pull his chair round to face the screen. Gaunt started his commentary.

'I'm going to show you a film taken from outside the house I mentioned. I'd hoped to have a view from the air. It wasn't possible. You'll have to use your imagination to give the picture the right dimensions.'

He touched a switch. The motor whined. A curving wall backed by trees appeared on the screen. The film had been shot from inside a moving vehicle. Occasionally the image jumped, obscured by what appeared to be someone's shoulder. The lens followed the wall to a pair of tall iron gates. Gaunt froze the picture. He altered the depth of focus, pulling the two-storied mansion towards them. He magnified the detail till Hendry had the impression he was looking through the windows.

Gaunt stepped into the glare, shielding his eyes as he illustrated his points.

'The house is built in the form of the letter H. The upright bars are these two wings – both of them are self-contained. This lateral bar is an entrance hall – the servants' quarters are behind it. We're only interested in the bit on the left – the east wing. You can see where my finger's pointing – that's the room we want – overlooking the porch at the front entrance. There'll be nobody in this half of the house between six and seven thirty tomorrow night.'

He ran the reel back on its spool and dismantled the apparatus. Then he let daylight through the curtains. He was holding what looked like a tie case. About a foot long and club-striped in some shiny material.

'What do you think?' he asked.

Hendry spoke frankly. 'If your facts are right, I'd say you've got a good thing going for you. How far is this house from a town?'

It was a while before Gaunt brought himself to answer.

'Three-quarters of an hour along the Cologne *autobahn*. It's just outside a village called Odensbroich.' He tossed the striped case across the room.

The contents chinked as Hendry made a one-handed catch. He unbuttoned the flaps, spreading the case across his knees. The kit had been assembled with care. It was comprised of a flat shaft of tempered steel, the length and breadth of a school ruler. One end was bevelled. A small, high-geared drill with an assortment of bits. A pair of blunt-nosed surgical forceps and pencil flashlight completed the outfit.

Gaunt's eye was gloomy. 'I thought you'd look a little more enthusiastic. You've got exactly the same selection of tools they produced as evidence at the Old Bailey.'

Hendry grinned wryly. 'Straight from the Burglar's Manual,' he acknowledged. 'Only those tools weren't mine.'

Gaunt's voice was patient. 'What else do you need?'

Hendry weighed the small jemmy in his palm.

'The safe key. You said you could get an impression.'

Gaunt's glance shifted to the clock then back to Hendry. 'It'll be here.'

Hendry refastened the flat case. Gaunt's assumption of

expertise was too easy. He was the skilled surgeon checking the clamps and scalpels before allowing some student to perform a minor operation. A touch of resentment leaked into Hendry's voice.

'I ought to tell you something – safe keys are milled to precise limits. There's barely any tolerance. If you're cutting a blank from an original you stand or fall on the sharpness of your impression. And nobody since Raffles runs around pushing keys into soap or wax.'

Gaunt nodded. 'What about cuttlefish bone?'

Hendry conceded the point with reluctance.

'You'd still need an expert.' He used the door key as illustration, laying it flat on a piece of paper. He pressed the wards down firmly then turned them so that the reverse side was uppermost. He pressed again. Last of all, he upended the key and left a clear imprint of the barrel in the paper. He looked at Gaunt narrowly. 'Three ways, not one – or you're wasting your time.'

Gaunt had followed the performance with interest.

'I don't think you'll be disappointed, Hendry. If the key doesn't work, you can tell me why. We'll have twenty-four hours to make an adjustment.'

Hendry's eyes narrowed. 'How do you mean, twenty-four hours? I thought you said tonight.'

Gaunt moved from the window. He stood by Hendry's chair.

'Tonight's a dress rehearsal. All I want you to do is open the safe and shut it again. Don't touch a thing – this is essential. Do you understand why?'

Hendry flexed his arms. This was skating on home ice. What could Gaunt know about standing in some darkened bedroom with a jewel box in your hand? Maybe only half the loot you expected to find was there. Because the owner was wearing the most valuable pieces on her throat or fingers – miles away. So you returned the box to its hiding-place, knowing that some day soon you'd be back for the lot. The refusal to compromise – the feeling of power and certainty afforded a special God's-eye view of the operation. And it was something you didn't acquire by reading a rehash of burglars' *modus operandi.*

'I think so,' he said quietly. 'I've been at this lark for a long time.'

Gaunt's mouth widened. 'Yes,' he said. 'Yes, of course you have.' He cleared the table, spreading out a large-scale ordnance map. Haus Odensbroich was marked clearly. It stood in an expanse of parkland on the outskirts of a village. Every copse, path and gradient in the area was indicated in detail. Gaunt's hand described the route from the city. The village was roughly halfway between Cologne and Dusseldorf. He tested Hendry's reading of the map again and again. Finally he was satisfied with the accuracy of the Canadian's answers. He folded the line-backed chart, looking at the clock.

'Time's getting on – we'd better have some food.'

Hendry followed him into the kitchen. Gaunt's cooking was unpretentious. He bent over a pan filled with eggs and ham, indifferent to the smoking fat. The two men ate without conversation, passing one another bread and salt with incongruous courtesy. When they were done, Gaunt dropped the dirty dishes into a sinkful of hot water. The clock was still worrying him. He checked the hour against his watch and went into the living-room. Back to Hendry, he stayed at the window, staring down at the street.

Hendry took a seat on the sofa. His stomach was replete but he felt none of the well-being that should go with it. Suddenly he could take Gaunt's tapping on the glass no longer.

'For God's sake knock that off,' he said loudly. 'Don't you ever relax?'

Gaunt turned round. The outburst seemed to give him the decision he was looking for. His smile had all the false assurance of a dentist bent on a root extraction. He lifted the phone from its stand, holding it out to the Canadian.

'Telephone the airport – ask for Passenger Inquiries.'

Hendry gauged the distance to the front door. He could think of nothing but Bernadette. She'd arrived. This was Gaunt's way of saying that he knew it. He wasted time finding the number – spun the dial slowly. The line clicked into action. Gaunt put his hand over the mouthpiece. The smile was forgotten and his words came in a rush.

'Use your best German. You're inquiring about a Geoffrey Long – passenger from Manchester to Dusseldorf. Find out if he was on the plane.'

Hendry relayed the request. A girl's voice dealt with his inquiry. He mouthed her question to Gaunt. 'Via Hamburg?' Gaunt nodded. There was a moment's silence. A man's voice came on the wire. Hendry frowned. 'They want me to hang on.'

Gaunt moved swiftly. He took the instrument, turned the dial several times and replaced the receiver. Hendry watched impassively. The manœuvre was a familiar one. The last spins of the dial destroyed the record of the call. Now it could never be traced to Gaunt's apartment.

Hendry stared across the small table. 'Trouble?'

Gaunt's face had lost colour. He fastened the three buttons on his black jacket. 'Get your overcoat, we're going to the airport.'

Hendry stood where he was. 'For what? That place is lousy with cops. I don't like putting myself on show without a reason.'

Gaunt caught his sleeve. The Englishman's narrow face was hostile.

'You've *got* your reason. Just do as you're told.'

He stopped at the bottom of the stairs, peering through plate glass at the street. The only person in sight was a boy wheeling a bicycle from the front of the school.

'Wait here,' said Gaunt. He disappeared through a door at the end of the hallway. A minute later the garage shutters were rolled up. A Volkswagen stuttered up the ramp and stopped in front of the apartment building.

Hendry ran down the steps. Gaunt heaved himself into the passenger seat.

'You drive. If anyone stops us, the car's hired from Karl Voss, Heinrich Strasse. The papers are in the rack. There's a licence there in your name.'

He put his weight on the gear lever, demonstrating the shift into reverse.

Hendry raced the motor. He was wrong. Gaunt had no interest in Bernadette. It was the man Long who was worrying him.

'It's easier on everyone if I know what I'm doing,' he said tentatively.

Gaunt nodded, pointing ahead. 'Just drive the car. If I need advice I'll ask for it. Take the first on your right then first left. Once you get to Graf Recke Strasse, Lohausen's signposted all the way.'

They made fast time out to the airport. Beyond the checkpoint, Hendry pulled into the lot at the side of the main building. Gaunt's words were lost in the scream of the Comet out on the tarmac. Hendry wound up his window.

'I want to know what happened to Long,' Gaunt repeated.

What happened to Long? The phrase irritated like an advertising slogan.

'Why didn't you give them a chance to tell you on the phone? Maybe he was never on the plane.'

Gaunt's mouth snapped open. 'He was on it all right. Try everyone. Porters, the bank. It's possible he took a car from here. Ask at the hire desk.'

The Comet was airborne, wheeling south towards the Rhine. Hendry watched it into the cloud. *You may now unfasten your seat belts and smoke.* In a little while there'd be drinks and a tray of food. A couple of hours and the jet would be whining into Spain. You'd get out, blinking in hot sunshine – a thousand miles from trouble.

He pulled himself together. 'You'd better tell me what he looks like. Another clergyman?' The gibe was pointless but so was the rest of the production.

Gaunt let it go. 'He's fat and he's English. Do your best with that.'

The large hall echoed with flight announcements. Behind the glass screen surrounding the customs bay, disembarking passengers were waiting for their baggage.

The usual complement of lovers huddled on benches, clutching hands. A couple of policemen were chatting near the bank counter. The flight number was up on the Arrival Board. Manchester-Hamburg-Dusseldorf. The plane had touched down on time.

Hendry walked over to the news-stand and bought a paper. He was suddenly alert to unknown danger and wanted to run. All he had to do was purchase a ticket and go through the barrier. Once in the Departure Zone he'd be safe. Then he remembered the passport locked in his hotel room. Anyhow Bernadette was already on her way. There was nowhere to go till this thing was over. If he tried running, the bastards would be breathing down his neck for the rest of his life.

He strolled to the desk on his left. A blond, scrubbed youngster in uniform met him with a smile. Hendry's German came fluently.

'I'm supposed to meet an English friend. I'm a little late. A Herr Geoffrey Long. He was coming from Manchester on this morning's flight. Can you tell me if he arrived?'

He knew as soon as he spoke that his question had impact. The youngster was staring as if Hendry were the link with some secret excitement. He made the Canadian repeat Long's name in full. Then he bent across the counter, his voice as confidential as that of a family doctor.

Hendry heard him out then hurried from the building. The rain was falling in stair-rods that bounced from the asphalt. He jinked through the parked cars, running like a hard-pressed quarterback. He banged hard on the side of the Volkswagen.

Gaunt wrenched the door open. 'Where is he?'

Hendry threw the wet mac on the rear seat. 'You're not going to like this. Long poked his nose into a transit lounge in Hamburg. They radioed the plane half-way here. Two confirmed smallpox cases were in the lounge. The whole of the flight's in the Grafenberger Isolation Hospital.'

Gaunt wiped the inside of his window, looking back at the airport buildings. The entrance was wet and deserted.

'Did they ask for your name or address?'

Hendry started the motor. 'If they did I was long gone. I left in a hurry. Where to?'

It seemed difficult for Gaunt to answer. 'Back to the flat.'

It was not yet five but the lights on Karl Mueller Strasse were already burning. They left the Volkswagen on the street. Gaunt led the way in. He stopped at each landing, listening. The top floor was in darkness. He put an ear against his own door – opened it as if he expected retribution to strike from the silent hallway. He switched on the light inside and drew every curtain in the apartment. The sound of his coughing in the bathroom was loud.

Hendry slumped in his chair. An hour ago, he'd been buoyed on hope and excitement. Now both were dissipated by something Gaunt didn't want to talk about.

Gaunt came back to the sitting-room. He sat down, his breathing shallow and quick.

'We're in trouble – serious trouble. Long has the key to the safe.'

The life seemed to leave Hendry's arms. The news stunned like a lead weight. The issue had always seemed clear. His freedom depended on two things – the will and ability to open the safe. Now the scheme failed through no fault of his. The cell on A/3 was suddenly very close. The man who faced him dispensed no favours. Gaunt's idea of a bargain was value received.

He tried to sound optimistic. His only chance was to keep this thing going – to hold Gaunt's enthusiasm.

'The hell with the key. We can blow it. We'll need gelignite and detonators. If you can't get them, I can.' There'd be stone quarries in the area. Security measures rarely varied. A wooden shack full of explosives would be protected by a dollar padlock.

Gaunt selected a plan of the city from the maps at his feet. 'People are living in Haus Odensbroich. I don't care about them but I want you to come out of it alive. We'll have to get the key from Long.'

Hendry shrugged. 'You must be out of your mind. What are you going to do – walk into an isolation hospital and ask to have a chat with a smallpox suspect?'

Gaunt's head bent over the coloured chart. He followed his

finger to the expanse of green in the top, right-hand corner. 'That's the Grafenberger Forest – here's the hospital. We'll assume that nothing that came on the plane will be released until the incubation period's over. We'll have to do it another way. I know they won't let you see Long but you might be able to find out where he is. The room or the ward.'

The thought itself was a crawling carrier of disease. Hendry's mind bunched tight, rejecting the picture.

'Me? Now wait a minute – have you ever seen Asiatic smallpox at work?'

Gaunt stretched his legs to their full length. His hands were pushed deep in his pockets.

'Don't be hysterical. This hospital business is purely a precautionary measure. The people on that plane are under observation – nothing more. Long will be wearing his own clothes. That means he'll have the key.'

An owl flapped in Hendry's stomach. He spoke without thought of any consequence.

'I'm going nowhere. In fact, I'm taking myself off the hook as of now.'

Gaunt's left hand left cover. It was holding a small-calibre automatic. The silencer screwed to the barrel was pointing directly at Hendry's chest. He spoke from a hard grey mask.

'You've come too far to go back. I warned you a week ago you'd be out of your depth.'

The small round hole fascinated Hendry. He kept his eyes on it as if willpower alone could block the bullet. Instinct told him that Gaunt was neither insane nor bluffing. The room seemed to hold its breath as he made his decision.

'Don't do it,' he said unsteadily.

Beads of sweat gathered at Gaunt's hairline. He thumbed up the safety catch. He appeared to put Hendry's plea through a sieve, viewing the residue with alien eyes.

'I need you alive – I told you that. But I've got to be sure of you.'

Hendry's mouth was bitter with bile. This made no sense. He had to go on living as long as he could. He burst from a flat expanse of time with an effort to be articulate.

'You *can* be sure! I'll give you my word on it.'

Gaunt sat quite still, his expression assessing. He put the gun back in his pocket and held out his cigarette case. It was as though he wanted to put the last seconds beyond remembrance.

'I'll take it.'

Hendry steadied the match with two hands. He dragged the biting smoke deep in his chest. Gaunt's odd smile insinuated itself into his deliverance. He had no doubt that the Englishman would have pulled the trigger, reluctantly or otherwise. His surrender had saved them both.

Gaunt pointed at the lamp on the table. 'Bring the light over.'

Hendry obeyed. The Englishman's back was turned deliberately. One short swing with the heavy base of the lamp would split Gaunt's skull. His fingers relaxed. Something other than fear stayed his hand. He put the lamp on the arm of Gaunt's chair. He had the feeling that he was irretrievably committed.

Gaunt mapped the route to the hospital. His droning voice robbed his plan of extravagance.

'I'll drop you at the gates. You'll have to do the best you can from there.'

Hendry stabbed his butt in an ashtray. 'That's putting myself on show again. Isn't there some way of ringing my appearance?'

Gaunt left the room, returning with a pair of heavy-rimmed spectacles, a plastic mac and cap.

'That's the best I can do. With luck, it won't matter about your appearance.'

Hendry waited in the hall. The spectacle lenses were perfectly plain. Gaunt was putting out the lights. He stood in the darkened sitting-room. There was the tell-tale click as a clip of shells was fed into the gun. He might have been checking it or the weapon that had threatened Hendry could have been empty. He was standing in the doorway. His expression gave no clue.

'Let's get a move on,' he said impatiently.

They sat in the Volkswagen. Rain bombarded the roof, a

drumming invitation to stay where they were. Gaunt touched Hendry's sleeve. He transferred assurance like a priest in a confessional.

'We'll be back with the key in an hour. They're looking for germs not burglars.'

Hendry let in the clutch, wheeling the small car from the kerb. A S T O P sign showed at the main line dazzle of Graf Recke Strasse. He filtered into the eastbound traffic. Twenty minutes of steady driving took them to the crest of the steep hill. He slackened speed as Gaunt pointed to their left. A gate-lodge guarded a wet, bleak strip of driveway. The brightly-lit board outside the two-storied building was adamant.

ISOLIERE BARRACKE–KEINE
BESUCHER

'No visitors,' Hendry said shortly.

Gaunt's voice was calm. 'You know that – but your case is urgent. He's bringing news of your invalid mother – anything you like. Pull in here.'

Hendry turned into a lane skirting the high wall around the hospital compound. He trod on the brake pedal, his voice unsure.

'Don't blame me if I don't get past the gate-lodge.'

'I won't,' Gaunt promised. 'Do what you can. I'll wait here.'

Hendry pulled the catch on his door. The wall hugging the lane gave him shelter as far as the main road. Once he turned the corner, the wind was driving into his face – lifting the skirts of the flimsy mac. He plodded on, holding the cap on his head. A car topped the hill. Its headlamps caught the open gates of the hospital in a yellow blaze. As he came abreast of them, he moved sideways. There was no checkpoint – just the lighted lodge windows to pass. He did it hurriedly, aided by the buffeting wind, and gained the front of the building.

He stood on the steps, wiping the rain from his spectacles. Beyond thick plate glass was the deserted entrance hall. He pushed open the door with his shoulder. It closed behind him without sound. He was looking down a polished expanse of corridor. The closed rooms bore numbers – black on glistening white paint. A second corridor stemmed from the other side of the hall. Everything was hushed. He whirled at the sound of a woman's voice. A small, starched nurse was standing in the office doorway, watching him suspiciously.

'What are you doing here?'

He blinked nervously, conscious of the cap on his head, unwilling to take it off.

'Good evening, sister. They told me you could help – it's about a patient.'

Her busy eyes fixed on his wet footsteps. The water was dripping from his mac to the floor. She exploded into indignation.

'Don't you see what you're doing with your dirty feet! Come over here.'

She backed away as he came into the office, taking refuge behind a desk.

'He was in the hall, Herr Doktor,' she said apologetically.

A man moved from the window. He wore an eye-shade and a white coat. His expression was curious. He spoke mildly enough.

'Don't you know this is an isolation hospital? You're not supposed to be here.'

Hendry stammered an apology. 'I wasn't sure, Herr Doktor. You see it's his wife – I mean we came from Hagen to meet her husband on the plane. When they told us at the airport, she wouldn't go home.'

The doctor crossed the room, his mouth indulgent.

'And she blamed you – is that it? What is the name of your friend?' He turned his back, scanning a chart hanging over the nurse's desk.

Hendry inched nearer. It was just possible to read the chart. Numbers followed the names. Then he saw what he was looking for.

LONG, GEOFFREY ZIMMER 7

He chose an entry a dozen lines above.

'Hans Schreiner.'

The doctor ran a fingernail down the list, nodded and faced Hendry with a smile.

'You can tell his wife it's no hardship. A little prick in the arm – a few days in a soft bed and then home.' He closed the eye farther from the nurse. 'Perhaps it will be better if you *don't* tell her. Women like to think that no good can come to a man unless they are there.'

The nurse's titter was dutiful. Hendry retreated to the door. 'Apologies, Herr Doktor – Sister. Good night and many thanks.'

He had the impression that he was being watched down the driveway. But when he turned at the lodge gates, there was no one at the office window. He trotted back in the direction of the lane. All he was short of was a tail to wag, he thought. A dog, proud of a new trick learned.

He rounded the bend. The Volkswagen was nowhere in sight. He started to run, scrambling his way along the wall. A flash cut the darkness in front of him. Someone was signalling with his headlights. Gaunt already had the door open.

'I was too near the road. What did you find?'

Hendry rolled the cap in the mac, threw the bundle on the back seat. He draped his own dry coat about his shoulders.

'Room seven. It's the fourth down from the front on this side of the building. There's enough wire in the compound to fence Alberta.'

Gaunt nodded. 'I knew it wouldn't be too difficult.'

Hendry started the motor. In a game where the cards were stacked you went with the dealer. No matter what, Gaunt had a trick of turning events so that they seemed to reflect to his own moral credit.

The front wheels slithered into mud, taking their own direction as the car jolted towards the trees. The headlights picked out a wooded park criss-crossed by bridle-paths. This was the Grafenberger Forest. The lane dipped suddenly, with barely enough room between wall and beech trees. Then came the grassy clearing directly behind the back of the hospital.

They peered through moisture-laden windows. A barrier of fieldstone, sixteen feet high, towered between them and the hospital compound. Those branches near to the wall had been trimmed close to the trunks.

DONALD MACKENZIE

Gaunt's asthma bubbled in his chest but he managed to control the cough.

'Get the car as near as you can against the wall.'

Hendry engaged bottom gear. The back wheels spun on saturated turf, whining their distress. Gaunt jumped out, adding his weight to the shuddering effort. The car moved the last few feet. Hendry cut the lights and engine and joined Gaunt. They stood motionless on the edge of the quiet, dripping forest.

'We'll be able to reach the top of the wall – standing on the roof.' Gaunt lifted a hand. 'Take these pliers – we'll need them for the wire.'

It was all a little too brash for Hendry's taste – the enthusiastic amateur approach. They needed a magician's wand not pliers.

'How do we get back?'

Gaunt pulled his hat firmly over his ears.

'We'll work something out. You're sure you've got the tools – everything you need?'

Hendry shook the lethargy from his mind.

'I've got everything. I'll go first.'

He clambered on to the slippery car roof. From the highest point he could find purchase on top of the wall. He hauled himself up – reached down to clasp Gaunt's gloved hand in his own.

'Watch the glass as you throw your leg over,' he warned. 'It'll ruin you.'

They lay prone on a surface jagged with broken bottles set in cement. They were looking at the back of the lighted hospital. A covered way, thirty yards long, connected with a brick-built structure nearer the wall. Concrete paths skirted the main building. Coiled wire made a no-man's land of the weed and nettle immediately beneath them.

The two men dropped at Hendry's signal and ran to the wire. Gaunt held the flashlight as the pliers bit into the barbed strands. Hendry made his cuts a couple of feet apart. He passed each severed segment back to Gaunt, working deeper into the coil. He threw the last strand into the darkness. They ran for the shelter of the brick outbuilding. Rain cascaded from the overloaded guttering, pelting down on their shoulders and heads. Hendry edged towards the window then tried the side door. It was unlocked. He beckoned Gaunt after him.

Inside, an oil-fired boiler hummed against the back wall. The warm concrete flooring absorbed their wet footprints like blotting paper. The heating system was fully automatic. Someone opened a valve and set a thermostat. Other than this, the building would rarely be used unless a fuse blew somewhere in the hospital. Next to the window was a battery of switches and control panels.

Hendry turned slowly, halting as he faced the boiler. An inspection ladder was hanging from a burnished guard-rail. He unhooked it – hid the metal rungs in the bushes outside. It settled the problem of the wall. He came back to find Gaunt in front of the door sealing the passage to the main building.

Gaunt straightened his back. The bottoms of his trousers were heavy with water. Wire had snagged a right-angled tear in the back of his overcoat.

'It's locked – see what you can do.'

Hendry bent at the keyhole. At the far end of the passage was yet another door. Where it led was anyone's guess.

He shook his head. 'We'll do better from outside. At least we know which room it is.'

Gaunt's thin face hardened. 'You can't or you won't open it?'

Hendry found a piece of paper – creasing it into a flat spill. This he slid into the crack at the top of the door and brought it down towards the keyhole. After a couple of feet the paper buckled in his fingers.

'It's bolted as well. There's nothing anyone can do, short of drilling out a panel. That'll take time.'

Gaunt swung away impatiently, his shoes squelching water. They stood outside the boiler room, looking up the concrete path. The gloom was slashed with patches of light from the windows. Hendry counted down from the front of the hospital. The fourth window was in darkness. They trotted up the path. Hendry masked the beam of his flash, playing it on the framework overhead. The bottom half of the window was fixed. The upper pane tilted inwards, leaving a small opening at the top. Metal brackets on the inside prevented the framework from dropping. He put his mouth close to Gaunt's ear.

'Give me a leg.'

There was just place to stand on the sill. The pinpoint of light travelled over a bare polished floor, hovered on a sink and white-painted cupboard. There was a desk and a couple of wicker armchairs – no bed – no patient. It seemed a long way to the ground as he dropped beside Gaunt.

'It's some sort of lab – I must have miscounted.'

Gaunt dragged him against the wall.

'Think,' he urged. 'You must remember how you saw the numbers.'

It was useless – all his mind recreated was a gleaming tunnel – on the right, a door with the numeral 7. But something was wrong with the picture. Surely the stroke at the top of the number had been facing him – not slanted away. Suddenly he saw his mistake. He'd been counting from the right instead of the left. Seven was across the corridor, facing the room above their heads.

Gaunt cut short the explanation. 'The window.' He legged Hendry back on the sill.

The Canadian pushed his arm through the gap. The first bracket bent under his pressure. He changed hands and put his weight on the second. He felt Gaunt's grip on his ankles tighten as the screws snapped from the wood. He caught the window and lowered it, then pulled Gaunt up beside him.

The darkened room smelled of surgical spirits. He used his gloved hands like insects' feelers, touching his way along the smooth surface of the wall. A crack of light showed under the door ahead. He turned the handle gently. It was locked from the outside.

His fingers were on the metal tip protruding from the keyhole. Something clattered behind him. He spun towards the sound, probing the shadow with his flash. Gaunt had stumbled into the cupboard, overturning a test-tube inside. Hendry watched the unknown liquid dripping to the floor.

They stood motionless, listening for the sound of alarm. Then the relentless pressure of Gaunt's hand impelled Hendry towards the slit of light. The Canadian clamped the forceps on the protruding end of the key. The leverage was powerful. He turned his wrists surely – put the forceps back in his pocket and wiped his neck. His legs would carry him no farther than this.

His whisper was unsteady. 'It's all yours.'

Gaunt widened the crack in the door with infinite care. The ribbon of polished linoleum unwound as far as the hall. A nurse was sitting at the end of the corridor. Her head was bent slightly. She was smiling at some secret fantasy. Hendry was unable to take his eyes from the door across the passage. Then the tongue of the lock clicked back in position.

Gaunt's voice was barely audible. 'It's perfect. I'm going in.'

Every nerve in Hendry's body crawled. The last remnant of his courage dissipated under the prospect.

'You'll never make it. She couldn't help seeing you. This place would be alive before you'd gone a yard.'

Gaunt's hand guided the Canadian back to the window.

'The boiler house. Throw that main switch. Get the ladder up and wait for me.'

An age passed before Hendry's muscles obeyed his mind. He lowered himself to the path and ran for the outbuilding. He stood for a second in front of the control panel. He rammed the heavy iron handle flat against the wall. The light died over his head. He found the ladder and broke for the gap in the wire. Behind him, the hospital had the hushed expectancy of a crowded stadium. He propped the ladder against the wall, anchoring the metal struts in the soft earth. A sudden confused outbreak of shouting came and went on the wind. He sprinted towards the sound of breaking glass. Gaunt lumbered from the darkness, winded and spent. Hendry took him round the waist urging him towards the ladder. The Canadian was last to climb. He kicked the support back into the compound and dropped to the roof of the car. Inside, he snatched second gear. The Volkswagen went into a series of skids taking them from one side of the incline to the other. As they neared the main road, Hendry slackened speed. Someone was directly in their path, waving a lantern.

Gaunt's head was between his knees. 'Don't stop,' he gasped.

Hendry gunned the motor. The car jumped forward. The lodge-keeper leaped clear at the last moment. They heard him shout – the thud as the lantern missed the car and smacked into the wall. Hendry spun the wheel. They took the glistening curves of the hill at speed.

Gaunt sat up. He was still having difficulty producing his words.

'Do you think he got the number?'

'I know he did,' Hendry said flatly. 'We won't go a mile in this.'

His hands gripped the wheel tighter. After a while he pulled into a quiet, soaked street and stopped. In a couple of minutes every prowl car in the city would be looking for them. They hadn't been in with a chance from the gate.

'We've got to switch cars,' he told Gaunt. Mud from the Englishman's feet plastered the floor carpet. He leaned against the door, fighting for breath. Then he held out his hand, opening it slowly.

Hendry moved instinctively – recoiling at the moment of acceptance. He stared at the small bright key with revulsion. For all he knew, disease was already at work in their bloodstreams.

'I've got to go to a doctor,' he said suddenly.

Gaunt choked on one of his pastilles. 'That's precisely what they'll expect us to do. We're safe enough for a few days. I'll arrange vaccination.'

Hendry's stomach was dead. 'Safe?' he repeated incredulously. 'What about the people we come in contact with – we're carriers now.'

Gaunt shrugged. 'The same people you've been robbing all your life. Are you going to drive or shall I?'

Hendry opened the car door without answering. He sprung

the catch on the hood and fumbled in the bag of tools behind the spare wheel. An adjustable wrench was half-hidden under a pile of tyre levers. He squatted by the front licence plate, undoing the nuts holding it to the chassis. As he walked to the rear of the car, Gaunt leaned from the window.

'What the hell do you think you're doing?'

Hendry worked at speed, undoing the rear plate. Then he climbed back in the driver's seat.

'You got us into the jam – now I'm bailing us out.'

The car crawled forward. The headlights caught a clipped hedge, a wall – the curtained comfort of the house beyond. A hundred yards on, an apartment building knifed into the sky. Its flambeaux-lit entrance was imposing but deserted. The driveway forked, the lefthand turn dipping behind the block. Hendry drove in then cut his motor. The Volkswagen rolled down the incline. Half a dozen cars were parked on the concourse. He made for the nearest and unbolted the licence tags. He replaced them with those from the Volkswagen. He locked the new set on their own car and took his place behind the wheel.

Gaunt was querulous and peaked.

'You've wasted valuable time. Let's not repeat the performance.'

Hendry looked up slowly, needled by the clipped sarcasm. He'd taken enough for one night.

'Didn't your little book tell you? The cops are looking for a number not a car. Someone here's going to have a lot of trouble in the morning. The next thing is to get this crate off the streets.'

It was twenty minutes' drive to the Brehmplatz. Hendry recognized the flat-iron building facing the ice stadium. Lights picked out each story of the multiple garage. Behind the gas pumps were the ramps and elevators. He pulled the Volkswagen to the kerb.

'Do you want to get out here?'

Gaunt pulled his coat collar up to his ears.

'I think I'll stay. You do the talking.'

They drove to the office at the foot of the ramp. The man

inside detached himself from his newspaper. He stamped par-
ticulars on a card and gave it to Hendry.

'A week, mein herr? Straight on.'

Green lights flashed, guiding Hendry to a bay reserved for
long-term parking. An attendant walked out, wiping his hands
on a rag. He waved the Volkswagen into an empty slot then
went back to his polishing. Hendry recovered the driving
licence. They'd both worn gloves – there'd be no prints. It
could be days before the law worked this one out.

The elevator stopped with a hiss of air brakes. They walked
away in the direction of the Brehmplatz. Gaunt's face looked
ill and tired under the greenish glare of the street lamps. They
trudged on.

'I promised you nothing but trouble,' Gaunt muttered. 'You
knew that at the beginning.'

'I've seen them come easier,' Hendry answered shortly. The
two men stopped, avoiding the spattered filth from a passing
streetcar.

Water dripped from the brim of Gaunt's hat.

'Is it smallpox that's worrying you?' he asked suddenly. 'I'll
give you my word about the vaccination.'

There'd been too much about the giving and taking of
words, thought Hendry. It was impossible to identify with this
man.

'Who did you expect – Fearless Fosdyke?'

Gaunt smiled faintly as though he must disparage a lapse
into feeling. He put his hand out.

'You've earned your sleep. You'd better stay in your hotel
tomorrow morning. Be at Karl Mueller Strasse, one o'clock
sharp.'

Hendry took the proffered grasp. He watched Gaunt into
the cab on the far side of the square. The rain had stopped. A
freshening wind whipped a hole in the cloud, disclosing a
sliver of moon nailed to the sky. He walked slowly back to his
hotel, trying to put the memory of an upturned test-tube out
of his mind.

10

THE STREETCAR jolted towards Derendorf. Gaunt sat at the back, clutching the shabby carrier in his lap. Half a dozen male passengers wore the same look of apathy – their shopping bags a common denominator of boredom. At the bottom of Gaunt's burden of bread, cheese and soap powder, the weight of the loaded automatic was heavy against his knees. He stared through the window at the streets drying in the morning breeze. Yesterday's sense of foreboding persisted – a refutation of logic that always irritated him in others. The success of his plan depended on reason – the manipulation of known human factors. There was no place for hunches.

The streetcar came to a halt. He jumped out and started walking south towards the marshalling yards. Dingy apartment blocks faced the trellis of railroad tracks. He crossed the street and turned into a dark alley. Mould grew in the cracked concrete under his feet. A corrugated metal fence barred his way. He slipped the catch and stepped into a yard the size of a tennis court. There was an air of desolation about the frame shack in front of him – the slack-tyred station wagon nosing the grimed windows. He pushed a door, sending a bell jangling. The interior of the shack smelled richly of leather and binders' glue. Dust covered precarious pyramids of books leaning against the wall. A cat crouched over a saucer on the work-bench.

A man shuffled from the far door, finding the light switch. His shiny head had a fringe of nondescript hair. A pendulous drop clung to his long, probing nose like a fixture. He seemed to shed the pose of doddering senility as he recognized his visitor. His shoulders and thick white face stiffened.

Gaunt put his shopping bag on the bench beside the cat.

'You look worried, Manfred,' he said quietly.

The German smiled carefully. 'Worried – Na! I had expected ...'

'Somebody else,' Gaunt supplied. 'Let's go inside.'

The old man held the door for the cat. It followed them into the inner room, finding a familiar hollow on the iron bedstead. A fat, old-fashioned stove thrust its chimney through the rafters. There were a couple of chairs, a sink, and cupboard – little else in the way of comfort. Manfred stood till his guest was seated. He groped in his apron pocket. Snuff browned the edges of his nostrils. His entire body shook with the violence of his sneeze. The last paroxysm over, he took the chair.

Gaunt rapped a cigarette on the silver case, frowning.

'You'll take your instructions from me in future, Manfred. Mr Curtis has gone.'

The cat climbed into the German's lap. His fingers went deep in its fur, kneading the animal's neck.

'I heard.' His English was slow but correct. 'I am sorry.'

Gaunt nodded briefly. It was as well that so many hands had worked on this jigsaw – each assembling a part of the picture without knowledge of the whole. The task of finding the key pieces was his alone.

'How many times have you been to Haus Odensbroich?'

Manfred's memory was precise.

'In six years, more than twenty times. It is always so – a telephone call – there are books to collect – pamphlets for binding. I deliver them with a report on Party organization in the Ruhrgebeit. Nothing else is required of me. I am paid like another workman.'

Gaunt flicked ash on the bare floor. 'A Party Card isn't going to help you after tomorrow night, Manfred. Only one person could have taken an impression of the safe key. Someone with access to the library – someone they trusted. You've thought about this, of course.'

The German's face was stolidly composed, his eyes unwavering.

'I am an old man – for as many years as you are born I have obeyed my conscience. At my age one is ...' he sought the English equivalent unsuccessfully, '... *verbrauchbar.*'

Expendable – it was a word familiar to Gaunt's ears. He answered patiently.

'You're wrong, Manfred – none of us is. That's why we're closing down here. There'll be money – you've earned it.'

The cat jumped sideways under Manfred's sudden movement.

'But this is impossible – where would I go?' He rapped himself on the chest, vehemently. 'Without me, you have no word of this film. Where is justice in this?'

An old tag stuck in Gaunt's mind. *Justice is the constant and perpetual wish to render to every man his due.*

Justinian might have been pushed to vindicate himself in an era of atom bombs and dialectics.

'Nevertheless you'll leave here tomorrow morning,' he said steadily. 'Burn everything that gives you a name. They won't be long getting here. Nobody's destroying you, Manfred. You're being shifted to protect the lives of others. A couple of years' time – you'll bob up – somewhere in Holland or Belgium.'

The German brushed snuff from his apron – his voice was disciplined again.

'You are a family man?'

Gaunt shook his head.

'I also. We are fortunate. Now duty – this came from London an hour ago.'

The cable was uncoded. 'EXPECT VISITORS THIS MORNING STOP SUGGEST WELCOME BLAKE'

Gaunt opened the top of the stove. He watched the paper curl, the white ash disintegrate in the draught.

'Where is your phone?'

The old man pointed at the outer room. Gaunt dialled the Hotelbureau opposite the Hauptbahnhof.

'I'm trying to find some friends – I'm not sure which hotels they'd be staying at. Possibly you can help. Yes, I can – Mrs Bernadette Jeffries and Mr Philip Proctor.' It was a few minutes before he had his answer. He put the phone down. The uneasiness that had invaded sleep and consciousness was

91

resolved to a single problem. It was better so but he would need boldness in its handling.

He walked over to the dirty window. The sign on the panelling of the battered station wagon had long since faded. He spoke over his shoulder.

'Is this what you use when you go to Odensbroich?'

'Jawohl.' The old man opened the yard door. The back seats had long been ripped from their shells. Pamphlets littered the floor. Gaunt climbed behind the steering wheel. The motor caught the first kick of the starter. The oil-gauge needle was steady.

The German nodded encouragement, bracing his legs against the cat's serpentine weaving.

'It is not a factory owner's limousine but reliable.'

'I'll take it,' said Gaunt.

Manfred ran his hand slowly along a battered wing. 'Ja – ist gut,' he muttered. 'So. Auf Wiedersehen.'

Gaunt put the vehicle in gear. 'I'll be back after lunch with your papers and money. Open the gates.'

It was gone one when he turned the corner of Karl Mueller Strasse. He ran the Opel round to the back of the apartment buildings. It was out of sight under the hedges of the tree nursery. He climbed the stairs to his flat. As he put the key in the door, he heard Hendry's voice from inside. He pushed the door quickly. The Canadian was standing in the sitting-room. He looked up from the map spread across the sofa cushion. His face reddened.

'You're late.'

Gaunt carried the shopping bag into the kitchen. What he'd heard was no trick of imagination. He slipped the gun into his jacket pocket, walked back. His tone was almost casual.

'Someone on the phone?'

Hendry's eyes were wary. 'A wrong number. I've been going over the route. The nearer I can get to the house with a car, the better. That wood opposite the lake – I could run in there somewhere.'

Gaunt shut the door to the hall. He sat on the arm of the

sofa, his silence a deliberate attempt on the other man's composure.

Hendry fingered the scar on his nose. He grinned uncertainly. 'I'll buy it – who did what?'

The curtness of Gaunt's answer matched his expression.

'I can get the number from the exchange – I'd rather you told me.'

Hendry's face sobered. He gave the thought consideration then squared his shoulders.

'You asked for this. It was Mrs Jeffries – she's in Dusseldorf.'

Gaunt looked at the carpet between his feet.

'Room 703 – the Breidenbacher Hof. It looks as though you're still determined to make a fool of yourself – even after last night.'

Hendry's mouth was hard. He set his weight carefully on both legs. 'You'd better get this straight, mister. I don't intend letting anyone come between Bernadette and me – you included.'

Hendry's voice and manner moved Gaunt to caution.

'There are two sides to a bargain. You're not keeping yours. It can be dangerous.'

The Canadian shoved shaking fists deep in his pockets. 'Dangerous for who? I'm getting tired of this Black Hand stuff. You people ditch your grandmothers and think yourselves heroes. I'm not a flag-waver – I'm a thief. I'm out for me and for mine. That's my side of the bargain. Do you understand?'

Gaunt nodded as if loyalty based on emotion could be understood. 'Have you got it all off your chest now?'

Tiny worms had grown under the skin over Hendry's temples. 'I guess so – just as long as I've made myself clear. Nobody comes between Bernadette and me.'

Gaunt wrapped his knees in his hands. His error of judgement had one basis – Hendry's infatuation for this woman. A smile – a lie – and she could ruin a man's endeavour. His as well as Hendry's. There was something ignoble in the thought. He spoke with awkward sincerity.

'We're much closer than you imagine. I'm thinking of what you said last night about friends. There's no friendship in a jungle, Hendry. I want you to stay away from Mrs Jeffries till after tomorrow night. Do as you like then.'

Hendry's eyes were puzzled. 'Philosophy isn't my subject. What have you got against Bernadette?'

Gaunt barely raised his head. 'Nothing. All I'm asking is for you to keep away from her for thirty-six hours. Don't even phone her.'

Hendry lowered himself to a chair. 'And if I don't?'

Gaunt answered without emotion or gestures. 'Then she'll see the inside of a German prison.'

Hendry's voice was quiet. 'I ought to have left you hooked on that wire.'

In an odd sort of way, Gaunt regretted both the threat and the reaction to it. Last night, common danger had produced a brief comradeship. But this was reality.

'Lives depend on what we do for the next day and a half.'

'You're knocking on the wrong door,' Hendry said at last.

Gaunt shook his head. 'I mean your life as well.'

'The man with the big stick,' Hendry said slowly. 'OK. We'll do it your way.'

One method was as good as another – the stick or the carrot – as long as he could keep this pair apart till Hendry's job was done.

'How much have you told her?' Gaunt asked quietly.

The edge was still in Hendry's manner. 'As much as you've told me – for what that's worth.'

'Do you think she believed you?'

The Canadian's eyes were unflinching. 'She's something special – why wouldn't she?'

Gaunt wiped his mouth with the back of his hand. He fetched the newspaper from the kitchen – pointed at the paragraph on the back page.

'I've got a fair idea what this says – "sneak thieves broke into the Grafenberger Isolation Hospital last night. It's thought they were after drugs but were disturbed before they could accomplish their purpose." Correct?'

Hendry's face was impassive. 'There's a bit you've missed. Police Headquarters say the thieves can get vaccination from any doctor. No questions asked – no prosecution.'

Gaunt walked as far as the window. The top of the station wagon showed above the hedge. He called Hendry over.

'I think you'd better be on your way. That car may not look much but it's serviceable. Leave it in the village and walk – you'll be safer.'

He gave Hendry the small, bright safe-key. The Canadian stuffed a road-map inside his overcoat. His thoughts seemed to discourage him. He spoke almost aggressively. 'I'll see you soon. If anything goes wrong, you can set your watch by this – I never opened my mouth to a cop in my life.'

Gaunt's smile was tight. 'Check the oil and water and remember – leave things in the safe as you find them.' He stood where he was till the Opel moved beyond the darkening line of trees. There was much to be done before Hendry returned. The promised money delivered to Derendorf – the old man's papers procured. He was tired beyond the ache in his legs and arms – yet there could be no rest till the film was safe in his hands. He closed the front door and made his way downstairs, stifling the persistent cough.

II

BY THE TIME Hendry wheeled the Opel out of Mettmann the *autobahn* was a nightmare of speed and glare. He hugged the inside lane, facing the lights of the northbound rush. The station wagon rattled – the steering was lax but the motor ran steadily. Darkness was complete when he turned into the Odensbroich outlet. The hamlet that gave the house its name was no more than a dozen houses clustered round the yellow glow of a *Gaststube*. He pulled in behind the cars facing the door, watching the windows of the inn. After a few minutes, he eased himself out. Beyond the curtains, the radio was shivering under the relentless beat of a swinging guitar. He picked his way past the sickliness of a pigsty and on to a hard-topped road. He walked quickly, forking left at the signpost on the edge of the village. A mile on, he saw the first curve of the stone wall. He stepped into its shelter, his footsteps soundless on the grass verge. After a while the wall separated from the road, pushing out a hedged field as bulwark.

He used his flashlight cautiously, looking for a weak spot in the privet. A gap showed near the ground – the runway of a fox or badger. He bent double and reversed, his back and shoulders extending the hole. Through the hedge, he paused to check his equipment. Gloves, tools, and key. There was nothing in his pockets that could identify him. He tucked his trousers in his socks and started across the field, every sense allied with the night. The wet fresh smell of the countryside – the quick whirr of wings as a bird got up underfoot – the friendly obscurity surrounding him. The lodge gates should be a quarter of a mile to his right. Beyond the wall across the field lay the house. He was alone – the watcher not the watched. He moved sedately through the herd of curious heifers pawing the oat stubble. They lowered their heads at him, their breath sweet and strong. Then he was at the boundary wall. He took a short run, scrabbling purchase with hands and feet. He dropped among pine needles and took his bearings.

He was standing in a windbreak of conifers, facing the front of the house. Floodlights set in the lawn threw the façade into brilliant relief. The east wing was visible for more than half its length. He looked at his watch. It was twenty minutes after six. The windows of the room overlooking the entrance were in darkness. He started to walk right – towards the sound of running water. A stream debouched into a succession of landscaped pools, each with its group of baroque nymphs and fauns. He used the marble statues as cover to come nearer the house. The noise of a car motor being gunned sent him to the ground. He pressed his face into the soaked turf. The bright round eyes of a moving car crept from the rear of the house – stopped before the arched doorway.

He dragged himself forward on his stomach – climbing the shallow steps from the lily pool like a lizard. The car door slammed. A chauffeur crunched across the gravel and rang the doorbell. Seconds later, a man and a woman took their places in the back of the black limousine. It glided in the direction of the lodge gates at the end of the driveway. Hendry ducked as the headlights swept his hiding-place. The gates banged open and shut. He lay quite still till the whine of the tyres had died away. The façade was serene and beautiful. Only now, a soft red glow showed in the windows of the room that was his goal.

He took his weight on his elbows. Whatever the reason for the unexpected light, he had to accept Gaunt's briefing without question. He ran for a rhododendron clump. This side of the house was dark and silent. He moved the last few yards to crouch in front of french doors. The thin beam of his torch revealed shutters fastened on the inside of the glass. He tried farther down. Every door leading to the ornamental garden was locked and shuttered. A waist-high window looked more promising. The disc of light settled on a wall hung with tapestry – moved along the dining-table set with massive silver. The door on the far side of the room was ajar. He held the flash between his teeth, using two hands to slide the steel rule between upper and lower frames. As he started to press against the catch, he saw the tiny box set in the embrasure. It was lustrous with paint – an innocent-looking appendage to the glossy white wall. On the other side of the window was its fellow. The first movement that broke the invisible ray between the two points would trip an alarm. He pulled out the rule, heart banging.

Ten precious minutes had already gone. And he was still outside, like a boy-burglar confronted with a bank vault. He crept round the front of the house into the brilliance of the floodlights. His shadow followed him across the long blank windows and up the steps. His rubber soles were soundless on the granite. The heavy door was furnished with a modern spring lock. An iron ring dangled above it. He took the ring with gloved hands and turned gently. The simple latch lifted. He slipped into the quiet warmth of a long, lighted hall. He shut the door behind him, keeping his face to the baize-covered pass door. The sound of voices beyond was plain. The walls were hung with portraits of unsmiling men wearing heavy moustaches. He traced the rich smell of tobacco to a brass-bound chest by the open fireplace. A cigar-end burned in an ashtray. He navigated the hall, keeping close to the wainscoting. The strong plastic cover protecting the Aubusson carpet could mean pride of possession. It could also mean dogs. There were too many uncharted hazards in this ploy for his liking. The painted china handle turned easily. He stood with his back against the wood. A reddish light from the top of the staircase showed him the way. He took the steps, three at a time, swinging himself by the balustrade. Across the strip of polished parquet, a fire crackled beyond the open door. The light that showed outside came from the logs burning in the brazier. He inched into the room like a man preparing to jump, leaning slightly forward with crooked fingers. A wide desk spanned one end of the library. On the wall behind it hung an emblazoned shield. The cover of the leather folder on the desk reproduced the same armorial bearings. He opened it tentatively. The embossed heading on the stationery grew bigger as he looked at it.

CHANCELLERY OF THE
BULGARIAN PEOPLE'S REPUBLIC

He had the sudden sense of not being alone. As though Gaunt were standing in the firelight, waiting and smiling. The first shock ebbed, leaving him ice-cold. Every hint and half-truth took on new meaning. They put a high price on his liberty. A log collapsed in sparks, changing the pattern on the vaulted plaster overhead. The noise died in the long passage outside. He stood in front of the ugly Gothic bookcase. In spite of Gaunt's detailed assurance, it looked uncompromisingly solid. Carved panelling stretched from wall to wall, forming a base as high as his knees. Above this were eight glass-fronted segments filled with bound volumes. A wooden boss topped each division. He took a firm hold on the one nearest the window and pulled steadily. The entire section of the bookcase swung out from the wall.

The front of the safe was a couple of feet square. A switch was set in the concrete surround, the button snapped down. He was whistling softly through clenched teeth. Experience warned of three possibilities. Either the switch operated a light inside the safe or the burglar alarm system. The alternative was a dangerous combination of both. Safety depended on the correct choice. He thumbed up the button and ran to the window space. The photo-electric cells he had found downstairs were duplicated on each side of the embrasure. No one standing in the grounds could see him, concealed behind the bunched curtains. He cut the line of the light-ray, raising and lowering his arm deliberately. He moved back to the door, straining his ears for the clamour of a hue and cry. A shutter banged in the breeze – somewhere along the passage steam clanked in a radiator.

He worked quickly, aided by the light from the fire. The slender key was steered home, the fingers of his left hand an adjustable bed for the shank. He turned delicately, the metal wards a perceptive extension of his flesh and blood. The tumblers lifted slowly to a position of twelve on the clock. Beyond that, there was resistant pressure. He pulled out the key and tried again – force would only jam the lock. He gave the slightest lift with his left hand to the key's forward passage. Though sweat dripped on his flanks, cold against the heat of his body, his execution was unhurried. His knuckles turned – up, over and down – till the key had described a full circle. He pulled the handle. The safe was open.

He probed the interior with his torch. He had to memorize every inch of this space so that he could feel his way with certainty – if need be, in the darkness. There were two shelves. On the upper, bundles of documents tied with tape. The lower held a black-japanned deed box. He lifted the lid on a selection of rubber stamps – an embossing machine. There was nothing else. He closed the safe door – unlocking and locking with confidence. In his hands the key was as valid as the original.

He flicked the switch into operation and pushed the bookcase back against the wall. The gilt-faced clock on the mantel showed a few minutes after six o'clock. He took one last look round the library, checking the carpet. A tiny cake of mud from his shoes lay near the window. He threw it into the flames.

He felt his way down the staircase, wiping away the faint marks where he had trodden on polished wax. He stood for a while at the bottom, his ear against the door leading to the entrance hall. It acted as a sounding-board. Someone at the back of the house was singing dolefully. He followed his shoulder round the door. The ashtray had been emptied – the fire replenished. He backed away, till he felt the latch against his shoulder blades. Then the damp wind outside was cold on his face.

He ran for the nearest cover and lay, his mouth inches from the surface of the pool. He looked at the house with triumph. Anyone less skilled would have been flat on his back somewhere in there – half a dozen servants sitting on his head. A moment's doubt tinged his satisfaction. Suppose that was what Gaunt had intended. The Englishman's briefing wouldn't have earned the tipsters' ten per cent in a thieves' market. There were too many important omissions. The next time he came here the front door could well be bolted and barred. Yet in spite of everything, the key fitted. Gaunt was part of the same system that accepted a phoney conviction, indifferent to everything but its own inscrutable ends. A system that dumped a man in this remote parkland, leaving him like a blind pickpocket with his hand in a policewoman's purse. Gaunt's version of the Old Pals' Act was too slick.

He rolled over at the sound of the slamming lodge gates. The limousine ghosted up the driveway and stopped in front of the house. He watched the squat man hurry through the front door. The woman followed – a few minutes later, the lights came on in the library. Somebody drew the curtains. He pulled his trousers out of his socks and trotted towards the wall. It was just possible that other people were out of their depth too.

He retraced his steps to the village, hurrying in the light rain that had started to fall. Much more of this weather and he'd be growing webbed toes. He crossed his fingers mentally at the affront to the Fate Sisters. A couple of weeks ago he'd been a con in a cell. Ahead of him twelve years of sordid skirmishing to keep self-respect and sanity. A nightmare punctuated by Salvation Army concerts, spring mornings seen through the high, barred windows of a punishment cell. The strange letter distributed each Christmas Day – written in Bible School longhand with the fiery bits blocked out in red ink. *The Wages of Sin is Death*. A reminder that justice was an axe in the back of the neck. Two weeks ago he would have bartered his chances of a Ring-a-ding Heaven for some lava rock in the sea and freedom. And all he did now was bitch about rain and hard luck. Funny. As for Gaunt, it was hard to figure anyone like that. These guys lived in a world of their own – where mysterious strangers received messages passing them on to other strangers, equally mysterious. You didn't take them seriously unless you were involved. Then you knew this was no B movie script but a desperate drifting venture. And all around complacent hordes went on punching time-clocks, raising cattle or shylocking their neighbour out of his heritage. Only people like Gaunt and the politicians knew what the score was.

A couple more cars had been parked outside the village inn. The other side of the door the guests were merry. He taped his satchel of tools securely to the back axle of the station wagon. There was always the possibility of some hard-nosed cop poking around on the heels of a traffic violation. He set the windshield wipers working and drove off at a steady thirty miles an hour. It was not yet eight o'clock when he turned off the Grafenberger Allee. He left the Opel under the hedge at the back of the apartment buildings. Karl Mueller Strasse was empty – the top floor of 118a in darkness.

He let himself in the street door, satisfied to stand for a moment with a quick sense of security. It was compounded of simple things he had almost forgotten. The cheerful bustle

101

of housewives preparing evening meals; the delighted shriek of a child; a violin played with feeling and skill. He climbed the stairs. The top apartment showed no signs of life. He was inside, his hand on the hall switch, when he heard the rustling. He pushed the door to the darkened sitting-room guardedly. The open windows on the balcony were outlined in the faint reflection of light from the floor below. The noise he had heard came from a flapping curtain.

He had taken one pace through the door when a light snapped on in the sitting-room. Gaunt was standing in the bedroom doorway. He wore no jacket and his trousers were creased. He put away the gun, running a hand through wild sandy hair.

'Don't creep into the place like that again – it's asking for trouble. You're early.'

Hendry shrugged. He pulled his legs up on the sofa and threw the safe key on the table.

'How about a drink – it's been a long tough evening.'

Gaunt rummaged in a cupboard, producing a stone jar of spirits. He put a tray of ice-cubes next to it.

'I hear raw smoked ham's the thing to eat with it. I imagine you'll make do.' He picked up the safe key – tapped it against his mouth thoughtfully.

Hendry half-filled a glass with the clear liquid, topped it with ice. He strained the schnapps down his gullet and looked up.

'A little surprised to see me, maybe?'

Gaunt yawned. It was obvious that he had just crawled from his bed.

'I've never appreciated that sort of remark. Just tell me what happened.'

Hendry refilled his glass, answering easily.

'There's an absence of warmth in your welcome. Just the gun and "what happened?"'

Smoke trickled from Gaunt's half-open mouth.

'I can survive without low comedy. I want to know about the key.'

Hendry clinked the ice against the side of the tumbler.

'Don't you want to know about the burglar alarm? The place was lousy with traps.'

Gaunt shook his head. His voice carried sincerity.

'So that's it! Every piece of information I've had about that house came the hard way, Hendry. Some of it's no more than guesswork. If there'd been no element of risk, you wouldn't be here. It's as simple as that. You're the expert.'

Seen through the haze of schnapps, Gaunt's insistence was remote. But Hendry knew that this man was not lying. The thought was welcome.

'It's a funny thing,' he said slowly. 'I don't even know your name but I think I believe you.'

Gaunt came back from shutting the door to the balcony. His mouth was wry. 'That ought to clear the air. Now tell me about the key.'

Hendry grinned. 'It worked – for me. It wouldn't for you. I still don't know what you're looking for. But all that's in that safe are papers and rubber stamps.'

Gaunt's query was studiously casual. 'You left everything as you found it?'

Hendry nodded, resisting the temptation to score a cheap point. 'A contract's a contract to me. You could have told me I was walking into Ministry property. It didn't matter too much. With every window belled, they leave the front door open. That's the gentlemanly approach. Burglars don't use front doors if people are in the house. The Rag Trade's a tougher proposition. The women pin their jewellery on the outside of window curtains – stuff like that. It's an attitude of mind.'

Gaunt smiled. 'Very edifying. I'll try to remember the analysis. And tomorrow?'

Hendry lowered his legs to the floor. His socks and trouser bottoms were soaked. The long muscles in his back felt as though he'd been in a bar-room brawl.

'Tomorrow's different. I want to do it my way. Someone in that house might forget what I've been saying and shut the front door.'

The idea prompted Gaunt to anxiety. 'Whatever you like.

The man you saw tonight had what I want in his pocket. There can't be any question of failure.'

There was a warm glow of well-being in the pit of Hendry's stomach. He thought for a long time before he spoke.

'Do you think I don't know that? We've come a long way from that room under court number one. You're getting desperate – it's in your voice – the way that gun's never out of your hand. I've àsked myself what could make it worthwhile.'

Gaunt's face was in the shadow. He answered quietly.

'A belief in a world without fear, possibly. I imagine you'd find that too fanciful?'

Hendry found himself wondering. 'It's high-powered stuff all right.' The moment impelled him to candour. 'You were right last night – I wasn't worrying about carrying smallpox – I was scared stiff about catching it. I still am. But I wouldn't have gone near Bernadette till I'd had my shot.'

Gaunt's dry mouth was flecked with fragments of peppermint.

'You'll get it tomorrow night. The RAMC depot says our chance of infection is infinitesimal. I thought it might be a good note for you to go home on.'

The long sweat on the parade ground was over for the day. The sergeant-major's dismissal definite. Hendry climbed to his feet slowly. You no sooner thought you'd solved the enigma of Gaunt's personality than he made a sucker out of you. It was the flash of the pea before a quick hand covered it with a walnut-shell. The Englishman was a real pro. Knowing him might have been worthwhile.

'What time tomorrow?'

Gaunt held the front door. He spoke in a rush as if anxious to beat his laboured breathing.

'Same time – and try to come in like an honest man.'

The small hotel was quiet when Hendry returned. His bed had been turned back, a plate of oranges placed on the night table. He undressed slowly, shedding tension with each article of clothing. He lay in the bath for a long while, soaking in comfort as he thought about Gaunt. A world without fear – it had the right sound all right. But like any other slogan, it wilted under a strong light. They were at you from the cradle with contradictory precepts. As soon as you had a hold on the 'Love thy neighbour' bit somebody changed the slide. Then it was 'War to end war'. You honoured your father and mother into the divorce court and saluted integrity in the shape of a windbag in Moscow or Washington. And even a joyless asthmatic like Gaunt was hooked. The most the Englishman could hope for – if he kept his anonymous head on his shoulders – was to retire and grow mushrooms. No medals – no public accolade – just faith in the millennium. They were all very high on faith and low on logic.

He wrapped himself in warm towelling – put out the light and settled under the foot-thick eiderdown. Sleep came suddenly, obliterating the last question-mark. A bell dragged him back to reluctant consciousness. He pulled himself up on the pillows, groping for the phone. He shut his eyes against its shrill insistence.

'Ja, Hendrik.'

Her laugh was a throaty catch. 'My God, Kit — That accent's pure Stroheim. Are you wearing a monocle?'

He sat very straight, holding the phone away from him. For as long as he could remember, he'd never heard her voice with more misgiving. He answered the tinny summons.

'I thought I told you not to call this number.'

She made a sound of exasperation. 'Don't be ridiculous. I've been trying to reach you for four hours. What did you expect after this morning – hanging up in the middle of a conversation.'

He hunched over his knees, resentful at falling into his own trap. He should never have let her know where he was staying.

'I've got to get some sleep, Bernadette,' he said carefully. 'I'll call you late tomorrow night – OK?'

For a moment he thought she was gone. But she came back, using his own stilted manner.

'I suppose you *are* alone? – How do you mean " *naturally*"? There must be some reason for this wild gallantry.'

He tucked the receiver against his breastbone – holding it

with his chin as he lit a cigarette. The feeling of guilt about this escapade persisted. First it was Gaunt now her. You woke from a dead sleep to find yourself in the middle.

'There's a reason. I'm tired.'

She took the news in her stride. 'Let me remind you of something, Kit. I'm here because I thought you wanted me. I can always go back.'

He saw himself in the mirror, snarling at her over somebody else's secret. His voice was weary.

'I don't want to fight, Bernadette. One way and another, I've had a bellyful already. I can't talk now – I *won't* talk now. I'll call you tomorrow night.'

Something exasperated her to vehemence.

'Now you listen to me – I love you. You're asking me to sit here for a day – helpless – knowing you're somewhere in the city, maybe in danger. Suppose something happened to you – suppose you need me – who do I go to for God's sake, the police?'

He sat with his head hung, seeing her troubled face. This too was part of Gaunt's deal. As if you could pin down human feeling with a promise – like a rooster skewered for roasting. Here in Germany, Bernadette was no more than a scared woman in a strange country. No matter what he'd said to Gaunt – without her peace of mind the plan was pointless.

He spoke gently. 'I should never have come near you till this thing was over. It's too late now. This is big, Bernadette and it's messy. Whatever happens, it's you and me. It always has been you and me – remember that.'

She answered quickly. 'That won't be much help when they fish you out of the river, Kit. That's all I care about – your safety. At least tell me where you'll be.'

Decision was a giant step that landed both feet on solid ground. He couldn't be anything but right. If he got through tomorrow night, Gaunt would never know the difference. If anything went wrong, she'd at least have a shoulder to cry on. Some other time the idea could have been worth a laugh.

'I'm going to send a key round by cab in the morning.

There'll be an address with it. The key fits the street door and the top flat. If you haven't heard from me by midnight – use it. There'll be someone there who'll give you the answers.'

She was quiet then her voice was an endearment.

'At least I can sleep now. I don't think you know how much you really mean to me, Kit.'

He accepted the possessiveness like a cloak.

'You've got grease on your face,' he smiled. 'And your room probably looks like a laundry. I've said it a million times – I love you. I'll be round for that key myself.'

He hung up and pulled the sheets over his head. Reality would be better than the image.

12

GAUNT WOKE with the initial caution of a cat. He moved no more than his eyes till the appraisal of time and surroundings satisfied him. He'd slept as he always did, half-upright, his back supported by the pillows. He swung himself to the side of the bed, tentatively inhaling. His lungs filled easily. The congestion had gone. Last night had been one of the better ones.

He dressed slowly. Clothes were no more than tools of his trade. There was irony in the thought that a man without that particular conceit should have a film-star's wardrobe – with a difference. The suits that hung in half a dozen cupboards from here to London were the uniform of anonymity. A Bristol bookkeeper – Dutch librarian – a Swiss office worker – any one of them might have worn the modest grey jacket and trousers he had chosen for today.

He moved about the apartment with the time-saving purpose of a man accustomed to living alone. What other people called home was a composite memory of a Norfolk parsonage. An upbringing as bleak as the surrounding countryside. The bewilderment at parents who disliked one another just less than they feared public censure had been well concealed.

School brought a deliberate choice of solitude – a conscious effort to be dependent on as few things and people as possible. Anything less was stupidity. For the next few years he'd done what was expected of him. The Cambridge scholarship cut short by the war; the Army School of Languages; two years with the military mission in Moscow. Since then, the end had justified the means.

He went into the sitting-room, pulling the curtains on a cold, cloudless day. Far off to the east, the skyline of the Grafenberger hill and forest was reddened by an early wintry sun. He moved to the window overlooking the street. The school across the way opened at eight. He watched the charging wedge of children, shutting his ears against their last shrill defiance. Marriage or its equivalent filled him with misgiving. His excursions into sex were hired or procured with no value other than that of surcease.

In the kitchen, he poured boiling water into a mug containing a tea-bag. It was a vile brew but the furnished apartment had no teapot. It hadn't occurred to him to buy one. He lathered his face, staring into the sagging skin under his eyes and thinking about Hendry. The RAMC Major had been explicit. They were hot smallpox contacts. More than that he wouldn't guarantee.

Vaccination *after* exposure to infection could minimize the attack – there was no certainty of complete immunity.

He used his razor in short, dragging sweeps that left the taut skin bare and shiny. He wiped the soap from his mouth and went into the kitchen, fighting the sense of frustration that lingered from the night before. There was something repugnant about a man bent on the ultimate personal humiliation – a waste of potential. Two days ago the Chief's theories on relative moral values had seemed out of place. Yet every attitude of the Canadian proved the paradox of a dishonest man with integrity.

He went quickly to the phone in the sitting-room. It was a mistake to leave Hendry alone – as if subconsciously he had sought to destroy the image of comradeship. The woman probably knew where Hendry was staying. She might even go to the hotel – possibly not alone. He could only guess at the part Proctor would play.

He spun the dial, affecting a composure he was far from feeling.

'Hendry? Listen – I want you round here immediately. Pay your bill and leave. It doesn't matter about that – you can eat and shave here. And hurry.'

He put the phone back on its stand. The margin was too close for another error of judgement. The only place for Hendry till he left for Odensbroich was in the apartment. It required an effort to finish the scented tea without choking. It was after nine – the clamour stilled in the school playground. There was much to be done and none of his tasks might be delegated. He went back to the bedroom, clearing the cupboards and drawers methodically. Every scrap of paper was burned then flushed down the lavatory. The bell sounded. He ran to the front window. The Canadian was standing on the steps below. Gaunt pressed the button, releasing the street door.

Hendry carried his bag to the sitting-room. The mud had been sponged from his clothes. Stubble blued his chin but the strain had gone from his mouth and eyes. He looked into the empty mug, viewing the soggy tea-bag with distaste.

'Fresh rolls and coffee, served with a smile. That's what I just walked out on.'

Gaunt shut the hall door. 'Why didn't you use your key?'

Hendry pointed at the bag by his feet.

'You said hurry and that's exactly what I did. The key's in my sponge bag.'

Gaunt led the way into the kitchen. He furnished the rudiments of a breakfast – fruit, bread, and butter – the inevitable tea-bags.

'Hold your nose when you drink,' he said dryly. 'It helps.'

Hendry sat down. He bit deep into an apple, speaking with his mouth full.

'I can't very well call you "Mystery X" – I'll settle for Bill – it matches your debonair charm.' His grin took the sting from the sarcasm. 'What's the matter, Bill? You still don't trust me?'

Gaunt straddled his chair. There were five months to go on the lease of this apartment. By the time the owner resumed possession, Hendry's file would be at the bottom of a drawer in the Central Office. A bald testimony of events, of no particular concern to the casual reader. But he would remember the man.

'There's something that intrigues me,' he said. 'You haven't asked once about the money you're getting – doesn't it interest you?'

Hendry put both elbows on the table, hiding the lower half of his face with the mug.

'You know where you found me.'

'That's not an answer,' said Gaunt.

Hendry put the mug on the table.

'I learned the hard way, Bill. You can trust certain men with either your liberty, your girl, or your money. Sometimes two of these things – all three together's almost an impossibility.'

Gaunt blew smoke at his feet. 'I see. I'm not quite sure how that classifies me.'

Hendry smiled again.

'You'll give me the money. I already know what you think of Bernadette.'

Gaunt was irresolute. The chessboard was set with the pieces. Hendry, the woman, and Proctor. And his the hand that moved them. The kinship with God was unenviable. He looked up, speaking with a certain warmth.

'I'm coming with you tonight. Once we're done, you can fly out with me. What I'm offering is something bigger than you dreamt of, Hendry. But you'll have to go alone.'

The Canadian shook his head. 'Ten years ago, maybe. I'm soft, Bill. I like a woman around the place. You asked if the five thousand pounds interested me – I'll tell you what it means. A few acres of sun and water – a dog, maybe a horse – and Bernadette.' He carried his dishes to the sink. 'Not necessarily in that order,' he said over his shoulder.

Gaunt watched him critically. He had a growing conviction

that after tonight a man like this would be invaluable. Yet it was a matter of time before the woman destroyed Hendry's trite exercise in sentimentality. A man blind to everything but revenge would be useless. Whichever way you looked at it, Jeffries was the stumbling block. Somehow she had to be warned off the course. Once she was gone, there'd be ways of leaking the news to Hendry. It would be easier if by then she had been replaced with the right sort of substitute.

He pointed at the bathroom door. 'You'll find my razor – there are blades on the bottom shelf.' He went into the bedroom, taking the gun from beneath his pillow. He went about his task mechanically – unscrewing the silencer, refitting it so that it locked on the last thread of the barrel – testing the trigger release – charging the clip and pumping a shell into the breech. He tucked the gun in the pocket inside his waistband. He must have made fifty of them – square calico bags that he cobbled under the top of his trousers. With his jacket fastened, there was no hint that he was armed.

He sat on the end of the bath.

'I've got to go out. There's your cash to organize – a dozen things. You know your way around. I don't want you to leave the flat till I'm back. I'll take the car keys.'

Hendry nodded indifferently. He was in front of the mirror, his face soaped.

'They're in my jacket pocket. There's something we've got to talk about before you go, Bill.'

Gaunt's muscles tightened. 'Make it short.'

Hendry turned. He grinned through the lather.

'Don't be so goddamed touchy. It's about tonight. Once I had the alarms figured, I got into that place almost too easily. It was all too pat. When you've been at this lark seriously, you *smell* danger. It was as though I'd been expected. With the safe loaded, this time, I want a couple of things going for me.'

Gaunt relaxed. 'I'm sure you've cracked harder nuts than this. What is it you need?'

Hendry joined him on the edge of the bath.

'I want to hit at dinner-time. That's when a house is more

111

or less predictable. The traffic's from dining-room to kitchen and back – you're good for an hour, bar accidents. I'll tell you what *sort* of accident – a dog locked in a room upstairs – somebody's aunt in bed with a bellyache. Anything like that can bury you. If you can see the place by daylight, you can work out percentages. People don't expect to be watched then – they're off-guard. All I need is a pair of field-glasses. You can leave me there, if you like. By the time you're back, I'll know as much about that house as the people who live there.'

Gaunt was impressed. 'Fair enough. I'll get whatever you need. I shouldn't be gone more than a couple of hours. If the phone rings, don't answer it.'

Hendry was more relaxed than Gaunt remembered. He followed into the hall, wiping a couple of stains from Gaunt's mac. His wide mouth lifted.

'I want you presentable for that bank manager. I'll take the money in dollars. Small bills and no series.'

The bank entrance angled the street corner. Gaunt stood in the shelter of a stone pillar, cupping his hands over the match flame. The Königsallee was busy with morning shoppers. Twenty yards away, a bridge crossed the ornamental canal. A family of sightseers hung over the parapet, dropping food to the birds that sailed on the dark green water. An old man with a beard sat on a bench, his face lifted to the sun.

Gaunt came down the steps, the paper-wrapped bundle under his arm. Two signatures had translated the letter of credit into the dollars Hendry had stipulated. Any one of the optical supply stores across the street offered field-glasses. He walked quickly, heading for the parking-lot at the end of Shadowstrasse. Pamphlets and cardboard squares still littered the back of the station wagon. He tossed the parcel of money in an inconspicuous corner. He sat for a while, Hendry's Canadian passport open in his lap. Whatever happened between now and tonight, the appearance of keeping faith was essential. The bargain had to be complete on both sides. Money and passport against the film. Only then could he hope for Hendry's future co-operation. The least deviation put his plan in jeopardy.

He put the passport back in his pocket and locked up the car. Small boys were throwing cartwheels for pennies outside the hotel. He turned into the passage between the two stores. Heavy doors isolated the opulent interior. The softly lit lounge smelled of scent and cigar smoke. Voices rose and died without echo. A fortune in diamonds rotated slowly in its showcase. It was a long way from Hendry's patch of earth and sun.

He walked over to the desk. He took the house phone, shaking his head at the clerk's polite inquiry. The call to 703 was answered immediately. He spoke quietly but distinctly.

'Mrs Jeffries? I'd like to talk to you – it's important. I'm downstairs in the lounge.'

Her voice was cagey. 'Who is this speaking?'

An American had come to the desk. The clerk moved nearer to deal with him. Gaunt put his lips close to the mouthpiece.

'No one you know, Mrs Jeffries. I'm speaking for a friend. You're supposed to be seeing him tonight.'

Her hesitation lasted no more than a second.

'I'll be down right away.'

He crossed the expanse of carpet, making his way to a table in front of the reading room. Beyond the glass screen, a man with smooth fair hair looked at him indifferently then vanished behind a newspaper. Gaunt settled in the deep armchair. He was facing both staircase and elevator. He watched the descent of the cage on the flashing board. There was only one passenger. A hatless brunette in a camel-hair suit. Her short black hair was swept sideways over a faintly oriental face. She stood, looking about her uncertainly. Gaunt rose to his feet attracting her attention. She came towards him, her long-legged gait hobbled by a straight skirt. He pulled the empty chair nearer his own. They sat with their backs to the reading room.

He pulled out the Canadian passport – letting her see the cover. 'I think you'll recognize this, Mrs Jeffries.'

She took the cigarette he gave her, crossing elegant legs at the knee. Her eyes had the black brilliance of new-laid pitch. She used them to inspect Gaunt from his fingernails to socks. Her drawl was unconcerned.

'Who did you say you were?'

'I didn't,' he said bluntly. 'I've made it my business to see that Kit's out of the way. I wanted to see you myself first.'

She twisted the topaz on her finger, her mouth hinting impatience.

'Why?'

The flat insolence irked him.

'At six o'clock this evening I'm going to tell Hendry who gave Inspector Pell the keys to his flat. If that isn't enough, I'll let him know he's been subsidizing Proctor for the past two years. You've got till then to get out of Dusseldorf. My advice is, do it as soon as you can. And take Proctor with you.'

She stabbed the unfinished cigarette into the ashtray. Colour flamed on her prominent cheekbones.

'How do you come into it?' she asked quietly.

He smothered the beginning of a cough – broke the top on a fresh roll of lozenges.

'We won't worry about that. You put Hendry inside for twelve years. Don't underestimate me – I can give chapter and verse. I don't want you here when he finds out. For his sake, not yours.'

She shredded the tobacco in the tray with her fingers. She raised her head slowly, looking at him with cold assurance.

'He wouldn't believe you,' she said simply.

He went beyond all pretence of courtesy.

'You bloody fool – don't you think I know what I'm doing? This is your life, woman, at stake.'

Her fingers felt the neck of the orange silk shirt. She made a mock salutation.

'That's pure *Kitsch*,' she said pleasantly. 'You're not dealing with some burglar's tart who's been told too much. You want me out of the way – it isn't going to work.'

He looked at her narrowly. There was neither the denial nor the fear he'd expected but a nerveless confidence he found disturbing.

'You'll find I'm not bluffing, Mrs Jeffries. Hendry's going to know exactly where you stand.'

She matched his challenge, her dark eyes mocking.

'As soon as you get up to leave, I'm going to start yelling. You won't get as far as the door. When the police come, I'm going to say you're carrying a Canadian passport that doesn't belong to you and you're here trying to get rid of stolen securities. I'll take a chance on the police finding them. You've forgotten one thing – the insurance companies are still offering three thousand pounds reward. I'll always settle for that kind of money.'

He sat completely still, hearing her cold certainty above the chink of glass and murmured conversation. Memory evoked another voice – Detective-Inspector Pell's droning recital of Hendry's convictions.

'... on that occasion, my lord, a large sum in securities was involved. None of it was recovered.'

The truth was suddenly plain. She'd never accepted a word of Hendry's story. For her, the Canadian's sudden liberty was linked to the missing securities.

He watched the growing triumph in her face, knowing that he was desperately near the end. Her threat was complete – the shriek followed by the lumbering invasion of half a dozen policemen. The smoke-filled room where jangling bells punctuated barked questions. She leaned forward, her mouth full and smiling.

'What happened – did I say something wrong?'

He shook himself free of the numbing panic, concentrating on one thought. Thirty thousand pounds were a greater reward than three. Greed was his only hope. He spread his hands in a show of defeat.

'It looks as though you'll have to name your price, Mrs Jeffries.'

The persistence of her smile was malicious.

'Tell me something – was this your idea or Kit's?'

He groped for the right answer – his shrug a non-committing compromise.

'He *knows* you came here this morning,' she decided shrewdly. 'He's too smart to do business with someone he can't trust. First he lied to get me here – now this. Why?'

As long as he fostered it, there was hope. This time he knew exactly what he must say.

'He got the news about Pell and Proctor last night. I stopped him coming here. I don't want trouble, Mrs Jeffries. There's too much at stake.'

He looked in alarm as she put her head back laughing so her throat rippled. She was suddenly serious.

'I'm glad – do you hear me, *glad*! I only wish I'd told him myself years ago. You may not want trouble but that's what you've got.'

He played her with the finesse of a fly-fisher.

'It's a pity. There's enough in this for everyone. By to-morrow morning there'll be thirty thousand pounds in the kitty.'

She let the bait float by. For a moment he thought he'd lost her then she struck.

'It isn't just the money any more. I don't care what bargain you've got between you in this. I wouldn't shed a tear if you brained one another in the gutter. I want Kit to come here in the morning – with fifteen thousand pounds.'

He started to button his mackintosh.

'For ten I think I could make him see reason.'

Her eyes were implacable.

'You do that for your own sake. Fifteen. And you can leave the passport. I'll be happy to return it to him. Kit doesn't scare me any more. Tell him I won't be alone.'

He hesitated then slid Hendry's passport over the table.

'Goodbye then, Mrs Jeffries.' He was careful not to stand till her hand conveyed permission.

She put the passport in her bag – taking the opportunity to inspect her make-up. She twisted the top of the lipstick, rolled the top half of her mouth over the lower.

'Goodbye,' she was equable. 'You wouldn't be hard to find and there's always the insurance money.' She pushed back her chair and walked away. He watched her into the elevator and out of sight. As he started towards the far side of the lounge, someone spoke in English, close behind him. He felt the hand on his sleeve and turned, shaking his arm free.

A blond, heavy-shouldered man was facing him. The boned black shoes and blue-striped suit were unmistakably Bond Street. He jerked his head at the table Gaunt had just left.

'It's about time we had a talk, Hendry.'

Gaunt's nerves were strung wire-tight. In the instant of turning, he'd recognized the man who'd sat behind them in the reading room. There were twenty yards between him and the swing doors at the exit. He had no doubt who this was. And for some reason Proctor was confusing him with Hendry.

Proctor linked an arm in Gaunt's, marching them back to the table. He sat down, clicking his fingers for a waiter. He ordered coffee, settling himself in his chair like a man whose only problem was his weight. He looked at his watch.

'Don't worry about her,' he said conversationally. 'She's got a hair appointment upstairs. She's late already.'

Gaunt's mind worked freely and fast. Instinct told him to accept the Canadian's identity. The beginning of a plan grew. It was no longer a question of escape but of taking Proctor with him. He tried for an approximation of Hendry's accent.

'The law?' he asked hesitantly. 'What is this – some sort of shakedown?'

Proctor busied himself with the coffee pot.

'Not the law, old man. An interested party. I've been expecting her to get in touch with you ever since we got here. It was a bit too neat this morning on the phone – the hairdo and so on – we'd meet for lunch. So I wandered along. Keeping an eye on Bernadette's proved profitable in the past. Sugar?' The backs of his fingers were thatched with fine yellow hair – their movement as expressive as any spoken cynicism.

Gaunt took the cup. He'd already underestimated the woman's quickness of wit. With Proctor he'd make no mistake. But he had to work quickly. He made his words an accusation.

'You're Proctor.'

The heavy folds thickened under pale blue eyes.

'So she's got that far – the big reconciliation scene with

117

me as the villain. Didn't she tell you about all those weekends she was missing? About the key I saw her give Pell – the key to your flat?'

Gaunt's voice was steady. 'I'm going to promise you one thing, Proctor. Sooner or later, I'll ram those lies down your throat on the end of a gun barrel.'

Proctor nodded easily, but a vein grew in the centre of his forehead.

'So she's got you by the balls again. That leaves you and me, Hendry. How are we going to work it out?'

The lights flashed on the indicator board beyond Proctor's shoulder. Gaunt forced himself not to look. Every time the gates clanged open he expected the worst.

'Stay away from Bernadette,' he said quickly. 'Or I'll kill you.'

Proctor stretched his legs as far as they would reach.

'You're a bigger bloody fool than I expected. You can plan a thing like the Benurian job – sit on the loot for five years. Organize your way out of Wandsmoor Prison. Yet the biggest bitch on two legs can make you eat out of her hand.'

He wriggled under the weight of his shoulders, done with an unprofitable discussion. 'Let's get out of here,' he said suddenly.

Gaunt showed the right proportions of alarm and surprise – the second strike had been easier than the first.

'We're not going anywhere, Proctor. I organized my way out of jail, all right – and you've fallen for it like the rest of them. There *aren't* any securities. They went up a chimney five years ago along with your chance of striking it rich.'

Proctor was becoming impatient.

'Look, old man, you're being a bore. Use your head – just count her out and me in. I'm not going to lose you till pay-day.'

Gaunt took a deep breath. He spoke in a dull monotone – the voice of a man beyond further resistance.

'I've got a car outside – we'd better use it.'

Proctor pushed some coins under the plate.

'It's taken you long enough to make sense. Let's get a move on.'

They threaded their way through the crowded lounge, arms locked again in a parody of companionship. Proctor was humming – the tune a link in Gaunt's mind to a time and place unknown. As they passed through the swing doors, the memory hardened. He saw the Chief's smile – *Abide with me – Hymns Ancient and Modern – good tunes*. He'd never know whether Proctor's choice was intentional.

It was a couple of hundred yards to the parking place at the end of Shadowstrasse. They walked in step, Gaunt's right biceps imprisoned in the crook of Proctor's elbow. They crunched over the cindered lot. Gaunt nodded at the Opel.

'This is it.'

Proctor unhooked his arm. He peered through the dirty windows of the station wagon. The inspection seemed to satisfy him. His thin mouth lifted.

'You go first.'

Gaunt unlocked the nearside door. Proctor pushed him across the wide seat, fitting his own heavy body behind the steering wheel. He was almost affable.

'You give the orders – I'll chauffeur.'

The hard line of the automatic lay along Gaunt's hipbone. His mackintosh was unbuttoned. He was sitting so that a simple movement of his hand could snatch the weapon from his waistband. But not yet. He'd no intention of driving two miles with a gun in the other man's ribs. There were lights, pedestrian crossings, where the casual glance of a policeman might discover them. Proctor had to travel under his own impetus.

Gaunt glanced in the driving mirror. The paper-wrapped bundle lay in the back, half-hidden under the litter, reminding him of Hendry's triple test of loyalty. Money, women, and liberty. None was safe with the man at the wheel.

'What are you going to do – turn me in?' he asked bluntly.

Proctor cocked an eyebrow. 'Christopher! Can't you get that sort of thing off your mind? We're partners. I've never been greedy. All I want is a reasonable return on the time and effort I've put in – a half share.'

Gaunt heard in wonder. Proctor's sincerity was unquestionable. All he saw in blackmail was a reasonable return on time and effort. Gaunt's expression was resigned.

'I've got an appointment with a broker this afternoon. You must know how these things go – he won't want to do business with a third party present.'

Proctor turned the key on the dash. 'We'll work something out. Where does this car come from?'

'Hired,' said Gaunt. 'It goes with some premises I've taken for a month. The owner's out of business.'

The blond man grinned. 'I always wanted to see what thirty thousand pounds' worth of securities looked like. We'll start there and you can show me.'

Gaunt relaxed. Proctor's driving was circumspect. He held the right lane, following Gaunt's instructions without hesitation. They forked left at the traffic signals by the bridge over the railroad tracks. Gaunt leaned forward, pointing at the narrow entrance between the two buildings. The corrugated-iron gates were shut. Gaunt clambered out, closing them again behind the station wagon. Proctor swung his legs to the ground, looking curiously round the untidy yard. As he took the first step forward, Gaunt pulled the gun. The elongated barrel sighted on Proctor's middle.

'You know what a silencer's for,' Gaunt said savagely. 'Put your hands up on that wall.'

The yard and the shack it belonged to had been well chosen. The entrance was almost hidden from the street – the iron fence hid what lay behind. There were no windows at the rear of the adjacent buildings. Beyond the frame hut was the blackened brick pile of a brewery smoke stack.

Proctor stood with his back to Gaunt, legs straddled, his palms taking the weight of his body. Gaunt's hands tapped the least obvious hiding places for a weapon. The key to the hut was where Manfred had left it, in the lock. He threw the door open.

'Lock your hands behind your neck and get in there.'

The colour had gone from Proctor's heavy features. He did as Gaunt said, turning sideways through the door to avoid rapping his elbows. He stumbled forward as Gaunt's foot took him over the kidneys. The fat-bellied stove in the inner room was dead. The bucket of powdered ashes was the last relic of the old German's thoroughness. A few sheets and blankets had been left, neatly stacked, on the end of the iron bedstead. The rooms were chilly and damp.

Gaunt pulled the phone along the work-bench.

'Your finest hour, Proctor. I'm going to dial the Breidenbacher Hof. When Bernadette answers, tell her you're at 14a Spielstrasse. Any cab-driver will know. Tell her to get here as soon as she can.' The safety-catch clicked as he moved it on to the red button.

Proctor's forehead was wet — his hesitation painful.

'You know her — there'll have to be a reason.'

Gaunt was already spinning the dial.

'Then make it a good one.' He passed the receiver across the work-bench, gesturing with the hand that held the gun. Dust streaked Proctor's elegant suiting. His heavy features were impassive — his eyes those of an animal trapped but still dangerous. He spoke with earnest insistency.

'Bernadette, I'm at 14a Spielstrasse — ten minutes in a cab. I can't explain on the phone but get here quickly.' Both men hung on the answer. Proctor blocked the sudden rush of questions with desperation. 'For Christ's sake, it's money, Bernadette, don't you understand?' He put the phone down, looking away as though caught in a misdemeanour.

'She's leaving immediately.'

Gaunt swung the full weight of the automatic in an arc finishing above Proctor's left ear. The big man staggered. He came at Gaunt, lifting one knee high in the air, then pitched on his face. Gaunt knelt, rolling the inert mass on its back. He pulled the puffy skin, exposing a pale eye turned upwards. Proctor was breathing stertorously through a slack mouth. Gaunt locked hands under the bulky shoulders. He dragged Proctor to the inner room, hoisted him on the bed. Gaunt worked fast, ripping the sheets to three-inch strips.

He rolled the blond man on his face again. Bending Proctor's legs behind at the knee, he tied ankles and wrists together in the small of the man's back. One end of a loop was fastened to the main knots, passed across his shoulder, across the throat and down again. The more Proctor struggled to free himself, the tighter the noose would draw about his neck. Last, the gag. He forced a pad of torn sheet into Proctor's mouth, securing it firmly behind his ears. He stepped back, out of breath and not completely happy. Adhesive tape would have done the job better. Still once more, he had been forced to improvise.

He went over to the sink, ran the flat chlorinated water into his parched mouth. The chance he'd taken a few moments ago had been deliberate. Everything depended on the woman's acceptance of Proctor's urgency. Her cunning was proven. So was her greed. Success hinged on which was the stronger. A sudden impulse turned his head towards the bed. Proctor was still lying on his side like a trussed chicken. Only now his eyes were open. They followed Gaunt as he hurried outside.

He stood for a while, considering the broken packing cases, the wet straw and weed that littered the small yard. One look at this desolation would surely send her scurrying for help or cover. He had to catch her at the gate – before she had time to think. He tucked the gun in his waistband and picked up a broom. He opened the gate, stepping into the dark alleyway. He started passing the broom over the asphalt, watching the street. A cab turned the corner. Fifty yards away, its right-hand indicator came to life. He moved back behind the screen of corrugated-iron, pressing himself against the fixed half of the gate. He heard the cab-driver's thanks. She was obviously waiting for him to go before she came in. Then the sound of her heels tapping on the pavement. The gate moved stiffly under her pressure. She took one pace into the yard. As she hesitated, he slipped behind her, crooking his arm round her throat. Lifting her bodily, he ran her across the yard and through the open door. Once inside, he put her down. She twisted as her feet touched the floor, using her knee like a street-fighter. He turned sideways, taking the impact on his hip. The jolt unbalanced her. He had her hands tied behind her back before she could recover.

He lowered the flap in the work-bench, trapping her. He was breathing heavily. Her flying heel had scored his shin bone. A nail-rake welled blood on his cheek. He pulled the gun on her.

'In with your chum,' he said savagely.

Her dark hair was tumbled on high cheekbones. The only colour in her face was in her mouth and eyes. She half-opened her lips as if she would speak. She was near enough for him to smell the scent from her cashmere jacket. Without changing expression, she spat deliberately. Turning her back, she walked into the inner room. She stood for a moment, looking down at Proctor then she sat on the side of the bed.

'Bastard,' she said with feeling. 'This time there won't be any mistake. I'll put you away for so long that you'll rot.'

He struck quickly at her fine-boned ankles, slapping her shoes from her feet. Forcing her back on the bed, he trussed and gagged her like Proctor, only the throat-lash he omitted.

He straightened up. They lay side by side on the bed – watching him with mute hatred. Her bag was on the floor where it had fallen. He tipped its contents on the table. Hendry's Canadian passport, a wallet with travellers' cheques. The brass tagged hotel ring bore two keys. The second was a Yale-type. Probably a cupboard in her room. He pocketed the passport, returning the rest of her belongings. He left the bag on the table.

'You'll have a long wait,' he said quietly. 'I'm glad you've got one another for company.'

He shut the door of the inner room. He made two phone calls. The messages were the same in content. Mrs Jeffries and Mr Proctor would not be spending the night at their respective hotels. They'd be back the next day. He ripped the phone wires from the wall. He inserted a sheet of blank paper in the old-fashioned machine, using two fingers to type the brief note.

MAN AND WOMAN CAPTIVE –
14a SPIELSTRASSE – HURRY

He addressed the envelope to Police Headquarters and found a stamp. He'd drop it in the mail some time before midnight. The letter would be delivered the following morning.

He looked for keys to the yard door – the padlock on the corrugated iron gates. The old German had either lost or hidden them. But the neighbours would have long since accepted Manfred and the seedy hopelessness of the bookbinding business. No one was likely to pry.

He drove the station wagon out to the street. When he parked on Karl Mueller Strasse it was gone one o'clock.

He sat in the car, watching the street and school gardens, placid under the November sun. The semblance of peace only accentuated his deep uneasiness. For too long now, he'd thought of physical violence as an admission of failure – no more than a substitute for intelligence. Yet twice in as many days, he'd deliberately used a gun to achieve his purpose. Twice, instinct had readied him to kill as if only death were the answer to desperation. Force had a way of rebounding. His own survival mattered less than his use to others. There must be no thought of failure tonight.

He retrieved the bundle of money from the back of the car and walked up the steps. More and more he had come to rely on Hendry's assurance and expertise – above all upon the Canadian's integrity. He pushed open the sitting-room door.

Hendry was flat on his back on the floor. His folded arms supported his head. He opened his eyes as Gaunt stepped over the ordnance map spread on the carpet.

'What kept you? I was getting ready to organize a search party. Trouble was, I could only think of one volunteer.'

Gaunt put the package on the table. He poked a finger through the paper wrapping, tearing a hole that exposed the contents. Each sheaf of twenty dollar bills was held by a rubber band. He tossed Hendry's passport on top of the money.

'I was delayed. Have you had something to eat?'

Hendry rose, pantomiming an aching back. He shut his eyes, groaning. 'Jesus God, I'm in no shape for this kind of thing. I've seen too many walls these last few days.' He flicked open his passport. 'Sure, I ate. You ever get sick of the sight of your own face, Bill?' His expression changed as he looked up.

Gaunt touched the weal on his cheek self-consciously. 'The car door. I walked into it.'

'What else?' grinned Hendry. He offered no more comment.

Gaunt put the passport back with the money. He stuffed the package out of sight beneath the sofa.

'I had no time to get the field-glasses. We'll do it on the way out to Odensbroich.'

Hendry stretched luxuriously. 'Hear 'em crack,' he said. 'Every crack's a month added to your life. Rids the joints of acid. My first Commanding Officer – a mortar blew his head off ten minutes after he said it. Ah well.' He drew Gaunt's attention to the maps on the table. 'I've been rechecking. I'd like the car nearer the house this time. This belt of trees beyond the lodge looks perfect. You can see where the track turns off the road. I'll be able to climb high enough to put the glasses on the house.'

Gaunt nodded. 'There's nothing for me to do here now. I thought I'd stay out there with you. I might be of help.'

Hendry shrugged into his jacket. He packed his tools in the tiecase. 'Not inside, you wouldn't. The house is no place for a beginner.'

'I wouldn't put a foot in it,' Gaunt said with feeling. He went into the bathroom and washed the dried blood from his face. He came back to find the Canadian standing by the window. Hendry's mouth and square chin were set obstinately.

'There are two things before we move. The first is that gun sticking out of your pants. I never went armed on a job in my life. Or with anyone who was armed. I'm not starting now. After yesterday, the idea alone makes me nervous. This is basic stuff, Bill. Leave the gun.'

Gaunt slowly unbuttoned his waistband. Without knowing

125

why he was content that the decision was Hendry's and not his own. He put the automatic in the bureau drawer and closed it.

'It's your show. What else is worrying you?'

Hendry scratched the white hair over his left ear. 'I'd say it's about time I knew what I'll be looking for.'

The smile was friendly but Gaunt found it difficult to answer. It was the moment he had always dreaded. The last shared secret that would leave him vulnerable.

'A spool of 35mm film.' The lie followed the truth without change of tone. 'Don't open the container whatever you do – the thing's not developed.'

Hendry was unimpressed. 'I'm not that curious. That's all – one spool of film? There's no chance of me making a boob?'

'No chance at all,' Gaunt answered.

They looked at one another steadily. Hendry turned his wrist.

'It's getting on for two. Let's be on our way.'

Gaunt stood in the hall watching Hendry go back and kick the money farther under the sofa. The Canadian's grin was a little embarrassed.

'Maybe you never heard of a burglar being burgled. It happens.'

13

THEY LAY as they had been left on the narrow bed. Proctor's trussed body was between her and the wall, his back presented to her. Blood caked the broken lump above his ear. He no longer struggled. His only movement was the constriction of his shoulder blades as he breathed. Her ears thudded to the steady beating of her own heart. She strained uselessly again, shutting her eyes in pain as the rough strips chafed the skin on her wrists and ankles.

Her first sick fear of captivity was gone. A fury of resentment had replaced it – a sense of injustice that this could have happened to her. Control of events had been switched through no fault of her own.

A nearby clock struck. She pressed her head hard into the thin pillow. Four hours had gone by since she'd walked into the yard – fooled as Philip must have been fooled before her. Ever since this morning nothing had made sense. The stranger at the hotel, Philip's phone call – least of all the arm behind the gate waiting to choke her into submission. The link between Kit's partner and Philip baffled her completely.

She lifted her face. Metal scraped on stone. The sound came from the yard outside. Someone was pushing the corrugated-iron gate. A man's voice called – uncertainly at first then louder. Feet scuffed over the bare boards in the outer room. The bed creaked beneath the frantic upheaval of Proctor's body. She added her own weight to the momentum. The springs sagged noisily.

She looked up into the unframed mirror hanging over the sink. It reflected the open door, the cluttered room beyond. A bent back was visible. Then an arm and hand trailing the wrenched telephone cable. The visitor wore the uniform of a post-office repairman. He lifted his bag of tools to the workbench, whistling.

Dirt on the bedroom windows dimmed the light. But she still saw enough to realize what had happened. This was no routine visit. Someone must have been ringing this number – someone who knew there should be an answer. The caller had informed the post office. When they failed to obtain a reply, out came the trouble shooter.

She bounced again on the bed, her cry muffled by the gag. The man turned, peering into the obscurity.

'*Giebt's jemand da?*' he called.

He came into the bedroom. Seeing them on the bed, his young dirty face grew frightened. He came a little nearer, muttering. Then he ran from the room. For a second she thought he had gone. But he was back, ransacking his toolbag with hurried hands. He slashed a blade through the tough strips of sheeting. First he released her then Proctor.

She put her feet on the ground, rubbing her ankles gingerly. The pain of returning circulation was almost unbearable. She got to her feet unsteadily, not understanding the flurry of excited questions. The youth's face was worried, not suspicious. Proctor was standing at the end of the bed. She was vaguely aware that he was brushing the dirt from his clothes. Before she could stop him, he'd grabbed the wooden mallet from the toolbag on the floor. He struck at the base of the youth's unprotected head. The repairman pitched and fell.

Proctor lifted him on to the bed. She turned her eyes from the boy's slack mouth. The impact of wood on bone had sickened her. She spoke sharply, hiding her revulsion with a show of indignation.

'Are you crazy, Philip? He's a child.'

He washed his face and hands thoroughly at the sink. He used the square of mirror to deal with the lump on his own skull then turned towards her.

She was suddenly afraid. She pushed her hands out to keep him away.

'What's the matter – what are you looking like that for?'

He made no move to touch her but tipped her handbag out on the table. He left keys, makeup and travellers' cheques and pocketed every cent cash money.

'Goodbye, Bernadette,' he said briefly. 'If you know what's good for you, stay away from me in the future.'

'Stay away from you?' she repeated incredulously. 'For God's sake tell me what it is. What happened?' She took a step nearer him, trying desperately to keep herself from shouting. 'You're not blaming me for any of this?' she demanded.

The boy on the bed stirred, breathing heavily. Proctor started for the door.

'You're in a class of your own – someone's back is always

128

getting in the way of your knife. Now get the hell out of my way.'

He made as if to push past her. She ran in front of him, slamming down the hinged flap in the work-bench. He cleared it methodically, pushing aside the jumble of telephone wire, preparing to vault the bench.

She blocked him, nails splitting on the rough wood as she clung to the bench.

'You can't just walk out on me – you *can't*! I've taken more than any woman deserves to take for you.'

'I'll take a chance whether I can leave you or not,' he said aggressively and landed on the bench with his legs dangling. He kicked her outstretched arm away. 'You bloody fool – you had to sneak him into the hotel behind my back and this is where we finish. Without a penny.'

She caught him in the courtyard. Once he went through those gates she knew she would never see him again. He *had* to listen. She clawed at his jacket, twisting his pocket so that his face swung close to hers. Her voice was near breaking.

'*Please*, Philip! That man who was here – you think he's Kit – is that it?'

His heavy lids batted. 'I know it is,' he said slowly.

She clenched her fists and struck at his chest. 'You've *got* to believe me – I never saw that man before in my life!'

His mouth wavered. Suddenly he moved as if her words had recharged his thinking. He opened the gates and pushed her out in front of him. The scene outside was caught in the apathy of late afternoon. It was too late in the day for commerce, too early for home-coming traffic. He hurried her to the intersection. A cab slowed as Proctor swung an arm. He paid it off at the entrance to the Volksgarten.

The pavilion was almost empty. They took seats at a table by one of the long windows overlooking the deserted park. A waitress left the comfort of a steam radiator to take their order. When the tea tray was served, Proctor took Bernadette's hand in his.

'I'm sorry. I'm the fool. Now tell me.'

She started with the phone call to her room – the unknown voice and its ultimatum. She found herself stumbling into repetition, the memory creating fresh anxiety. Proctor listened attentively, arms folded, his eyes impassive. She sensed a lack of conviction in his expression and had the hopelessness of expressing a truth doomed to disbelief. Then she was done. She showed him the unlit cigarette in her hand. He touched a match to it. Her cheeks were wet and he was a little out of focus.

'Don't you believe me, Philip?'

He was gazing through the window at the darkening skyline. 'Of course I do. What I don't understand is why that bastard let me think he was Hendry?'

She neither knew nor cared but came to what was troubling her. 'Philip – I told the truth about the hairdressing appointment. Why were you watching me?'

He turned his head, smiling. 'I was jealous.'

He was lying but she didn't care. She groped for something solid in a fog of conjecture.

'Now listen to me. Kit's dangerous. We've still got time. We can be out of Dusseldorf in an hour.'

He seemed not to hear, shaking his head impatiently. 'I've got an idea. When did you last talk to Hendry?'

She slid the heavy bracelet away from her raw wrist. She concentrated on the hour and minute.

'Last night – when I told you. A few minutes before I spoke to you. I tried the hotel again this morning but he'd already checked out.'

He nodded. 'How about the key he was supposed to send round by cab?'

She took hold of her handbag, her voice unsteady. 'No. I'll make this up to you any way you like, Philip, but I just can't go on. I'm scared, don't you understand?'

He forced her fingers open. 'Keep your voice down – the girl's watching you.' He found the extra key hooked to the hotel room tag. He searched the rest of her bag again thoroughly. 'Where's the address?'

She shut her eyes tight, shaking her head. 'I keep telling

you again and again. I know how Kit's mind works. This is a
trap and that man's in it with him.'

He smiled for the benefit of the waitress but his low voice
was savage.

'What the hell happened to you, Bernadette? Why have
you suddenly gone to pieces? Of course they're in it together
but it isn't as you think. That joker wanted us out of the way.
Everything he said to you pointed to it. When that didn't work
you saw what happened. Whatever he knows, be sure he hasn't
told your boy-friend. Use your intelligence – if Hendry knew
about me or about Pell do you think your head would still be
on your shoulders?'

In spite of his vehemence her fear persisted. She repaired
her make-up, using the time to find courage to give him an
ultimatum. She could only answer weakly.

'I want us to go – to get out of this city.'

He switched to warmth and tolerance. 'I know how you
feel, darling. But it's madness to let ourselves be bluffed out.
That's what it would be if we left. Don't you see what's hap-
pening? – Hendry's being doublecrossed. It sticks out a
mile. For some reason it would be easier with us out of the
way.'

The old spell was working. At any other time she'd have
laughed at herself and at him too. Now she was indifferent to
anything except losing him.

'This money means more to you than anything else in the
world, doesn't it, Philip?'

He shrugged and looked away. 'No. I'll go with you if
that's what you really want. You've probably got it all worked
out already. Some hovel on a by-pass – you sitting in curlers
waiting for me to come home from work. Do you think that's
us?'

She quelled the shake in her heart. It was important to
argue no more. Her voice was quite calm.

'Pay the bill, Philip. We'll do whatever you want.'

He smiled, smoke drifting from his nostrils. 'You're too
sensible to say anything else. I've waited a long time for this,

darling. Nobody's going to stop me now.' He flicked his fingers for the waitress, sharing his sudden good humour with her.

Bernadette gathered her things together. 'The address was in the envelope with the key,' she said quietly. 'I memorized it and tore it up. 118a Karl Mueller Strasse.'

He spread a pocket map across the table cloth. He traced a course and then nodded.

'We're going to put our money on the favourite. Whatever this house is, my guess is that it's where the payoff takes place. If Hendry gave you midnight as a deadline we'll be there well before. Now, in fact.'

She was carefully uncritical but the implication worried her.

'Couldn't there be someone in the house already?'

He pulled her chair away for her, tucked her arm under his. 'That's what we're going to find out.' He walked her to the door.

It was dark when they reached Karl Mueller Strasse. The apartment dwellers were already busy with the first chores of the evening. Cars were being put away, curtains drawn. A group of children scampered over the grass after a dog. They walked the length of the street to establish their bearings. She stood outside the phone booth, listening as he asked an English-speaking operator for his number. He held the door open, putting the receiver to his ear. The bell was ringing, shrill and unanswered.

'Dead,' he said softly. 'There's nobody there.'

They strolled back through the shrubbery. Behind the sprawling bulk of the silent school, he pulled her into the shadow.

'We're walking straight in and up the stairs. If we meet anyone on the way, remember we're not burglars. We're letting ourselves through our own door with the key. If somebody smiles, smile back but don't open your mouth.'

They hurried up the steps to the street entrance. Proctor's face was set and white under the hanging light. The key worked smoothly. He shut the door behind them and led the way. She was holding tight to the back of his jacket as if that and nothing else would protect her. They climbed past doors enclosing warmth and sound and stopped on the top floor. The landing was in darkness. She sensed that Proctor was bending down. The mail flap banged as his fingers released it.

His voice was no more than a whisper. 'Match.'

She held the tiny flame so that he could steer the key into the lock. He opened the door, stepping back quickly on to the landing. An impression of emptiness extended from the interior. It was even darker than outside. She felt his hand take hers and followed him into the silent hall.

The sudden light startled her. Proctor draped a table cover over the bottle-lamp. His voice was too loud – she felt he should still be whispering.

'Make sure that door's properly shut.'

She stood with her back to the hall, listening as he moved swiftly through the rest of the rooms. Every sound was magnified. She flinched as a curtain rattled on its rail. A closet door creaked. Then Proctor was leaning in the doorway, considering his surroundings like a new tenant doubtful of the furnishings. The very casualness of his manner terrified her.

The room was long with draped french windows at front and back. She watched, dry-mouthed, as he opened a chink in the hanging folds. He did the same thing at the far end of the room. He hitched the curtain back in place, walking the polished boards with no more noise than on the carpet.

'What could be better than balconies. Two of them.'

Suddenly her legs no longer supported her. She slumped on the chintz sofa, barely managing to speak.

'I'm ill, Philip – the bathroom.'

He stood wide-legged, looking down at her.

The expression in his eyes helped her back on her feet. She broke away from him, running for what had to be the kitchen. Her forehead and throat were cold with sweat. She hunched in misery over the sink, past shame, and vomited. She stayed there, hoping she was forgotten, till the nausea was over. Nothing had tasted as good as the water from the faucet, flat with chemicals but cold. She was tidying herself in the tiny bathroom when Proctor's call brought her hurrying back. He was sprawling across the sofa on his belly. On the floor beside him was a package wrapped in newsprint. An automatic with strangely elongated barrel lay on the table. His thin mouth was wide in pleasure. He pulled back a corner of the wrapping paper like a jeweller displaying his choicest gems.

It seemed more money than she had ever seen at one time. The hundred dollar bills were banded in sheaves.

'The best part of five thousand quid,' he said reverently. It was as if he had needed an audience to obtain the fullest satisfaction. He took the money into the bedroom, came back checking the mechanism of the weapon with sure fingers.

'This was in a drawer. They provide everything.'

She was suddenly disturbed. It was the sight of the gun in his hands – his assumption of mental and physical superiority. She tried for the right words.

'Why don't we take the money and go, Philip? Couldn't we?' she urged.

He settled back in the cushions, pulling away his legs as if the idea might physically contaminate him.

'There's nothing to stop you going. I'll give you back the cash you came with. There's the door – go ahead!'

She turned away, knowing that any answer would only provoke him. He wasn't serious. Everything he said and did stemmed from this violent jealousy of Kit. He was testing her loyalty with every taunt. It wasn't even a jealousy that mattered – but an assumption of superior cunning. She lit a cigarette.

He took it from her, crushed it out and hid the butt.

'They'll smell the smoke from the landing. What do you think the dollars are for, Bernadette?'

The truth was simple. 'I don't know.'

His eyes were remote. He looked doubtful whether or not to share some deeper insight. 'But I do,' he said smiling. 'They're the hook. The carrot before the ass. It's as much of thirty thousand pounds as Hendry would ever see.'

Hope leapt in her voice. 'Then why don't we go?'

He repeated the word with distaste. 'Can't you say anything else but "go"? That's why we're staying. He's still going to bring the bloody stuff here, isn't he?'

She knew argument was useless. Whatever the end, it was for them both. There was no other way.

He tapped himself on the chest. 'I've got contacts he never heard of. I don't need him to put the bonds on the market. That money on the bed's just an unexpected dividend.' He seemed content with her silence and started to prowl the room, poking and searching. He took out every lamp bulb, leaving only one in the ceiling. She heard him in the kitchen, the bedroom and bathroom. Last of all in the hall. He came back to put a chair in the centre of the carpet. It was immediately beneath the chandelier he had left untouched. The switch operating the light was near the hall door. He took her by the shoulder, pulling her down on the chair. He put the palm of his hand against her cheek.

'Do you love me?'

She lifted her head. His eyes were very bright – he looked almost happy. She leaned hard against his fingers. He opened the door to the balcony overlooking the street and turned round. His face was utterly confident.

'Whether it's one or two of them, this is what happens. The light goes on and you're sitting in the chair facing the hall door. For a split second the only thing they'll see is a woman alone. To reach you, they've got to put their backs to this window. Can you do it?'

She nodded. He smiled again, came near and put his mouth on hers. In spite of herself, she shivered. It had to be a trick of imagination but his lips were as living as rubber.

He swung the automatic in a chopping motion.

'We don't need luck any more, Bernadette,' he said quietly. 'Just patience.'

She listened to him, sitting quite still. It was no longer important to think, only to do as he told her. He switched off the light and stepped out on the balcony. The distant rumble of streetcars, a dog's bark, were the only sounds that gave time meaning. It was a long while before the balcony door opened. She gripped the sides of her chair, digging her heels into the carpet.

He whispered from the darkness. 'It's the two of them. They're coming across the street from the school. Whatever happens, don't move – don't say anything.' He closed the glass door again.

She forced herself to immobility. She tried to listen beyond the sudden blare of television from the apartment below. There was no sound that could be identified. But her ears counted unheard footsteps. Then someone pushed a key into the front door. The noise from downstairs swelled, dying as the lock clicked shut. She braced herself to meet the light overhead.

14

IN FRONT of them, the *autobahn* sliced into the distance. The grass dividing strip only accentuated the monotony of the four-lane highway. An unending stream of vehicles raced north and south. Beetle-like sports cars whined past grimly driven sedans. On the long ascents, giant diesel trucks hugged the inside edge, second class citizens in a realm of speed. There was no contact with the countryside behind the unending fences. The fields ploughed in chocolate furrows were thick with crows. Sentry birds dozed on the telegraph poles, contemptuous of the traffic. The forests were silent, scarcely penetrated by a sun that had no strength.

Hendry kept the station wagon down to forty miles an hour. The tyres hummed regularly. Now and again the exhaust roared as they shot into the cavern of an underpass. Gaunt had discouraged conversation ever since they had left Dusseldorf. He was leaning back, resting his head against the bench seat. The only time he opened his eyes was for a change of speed or a deviation from line. Hendry was vaguely resentful, conscious of his own growing tenseness. These last two days he'd lived too close to danger for the word to have mean-

ing any more. Yet those had only been preliminary bouts –
the main event was coming up. Yesterday it had been Gaunt
who showed signs of cracking. Now with success or failure
only hours away he seemed to have found a fresh source of
strength.

A group of buildings loomed in front, a twentieth-century
posting halt. Hotel, restaurant, filling station. He swung the
Opel into the lane staggered for emerging traffic and braked
in front of the pumps. Gaunt's head rolled, his eyes alert.
Hendry tapped the gas gauge. The needle showed the tank to
be a quarter full. Gaunt stretched.

'Why bother – there's enough for what we need.'

Hendry handed the keys through the window. He opened
the door on his side and walked round the station wagon
checking the tyres. He watched the fuel nozzle till gas bubbled
down the rear fender. He paid the attendant and took his seat
behind the wheel.

'The longest way home can be the safest. I'll be happier
with a full tank.'

Gaunt offered no further criticism, yet watching him,
Hendry no longer found the mask of indifference convincing.
He had the sudden feeling that Gaunt's anxiety was as com-
pulsive as his own. He put the car in gear. Odensbroich was
only twenty kilometres away. It was a little after three when
he pulled off the *autobahn* and headed the car to the village.
Gaunt had handed over leadership like a relay runner the
baton. Its passing seemed to have left him spent and jaded.
Hendry put the question bluntly.

'What do you get out of this, Bill? Money – promotion –
those things don't matter to you. I'm not kidding, I want to
know. Maybe I've missed something.'

Gaunt locked both hands round his knees. He was staring
straight ahead through the windshield. He cleared his throat
twice before he spoke.

'I don't think you'd understand. What I get means nothing.'

Hendry took it for what it was – a rebuff. Gaunt showed
feeling like a man displays shirt-cuff. A certain length was
permissible – the rest must be hidden.

137

They drove through the hamlet where Hendry had parked, forking at the boundary wall. Daylight gave the surroundings new proportions. Beyond the sweep of the road was the lodge. The gilt-topped gates were flung wide. There was a brief glimpse of cars and trucks parked in front of the stone built *schloss*. Gaunt's movement was involuntary. He twisted in his seat, looking back.

'Christ Almighty – what's that?'

Hendry kept his foot on the accelerator.

'This is no place to stop. We'll see better from cover.'

They passed the field where he had climbed the wall. The cattle were bunched, heads lowered, trampling the hay they were eating. A quarter-mile on, the road veered right leaving a belt of pine and larch between it and the wall. Wire circled the spinney, broken by a padlocked gate. Hendry ran the car on a hundred yards then stopped. He fished the solid length of jack handle from the litter in the back.

'Get the front up. If anyone comes by, your motor's giving trouble.'

He climbed the wire fence and ran back through the trees to the gate. Half a dozen blows with the jack handle cracked the rivets from the padlock. He undid the gate. Stepping out to the road, he waved. Gaunt reversed the Opel and steered it through the gap. What track there might have been was long since covered with pine needles. Hendry eased the car deeper into the trees. They were well hidden. The boundary wall glimmered beyond, its base black with weed and ivy.

He turned to Gaunt. 'This'll do, we're out of sight from the road.'

He pulled the field-glasses from their case, hanging them round his neck by the strap. They walked as far as the wall. Beyond its top the naked sturdiness of oak trees reached into the air. The pines on their side of the wall were deep green to their slender tops. He chose one. Ten feet from the ground, its boughs stood out at right angles, offering an easy ascent. There was neither movement nor sound in the spinney.

He clambered on Gaunt's back, grabbing at the lowest

branch. He worked his way to the summit, his face sticky with spiders' webs. The tree swayed a little under his weight. He locked his thighs about the branch. Sighting the powerful lens, he brought the front of the house near enough to be touched. Half a dozen cars were parked haphazardly on the concourse. Three trucks were backed between the lawn and the end of the east wing. He lifted the glasses slightly.

The library windows were open. Power lines snaked from the trucks to microphones set up on the grass. A couple of men were measuring the distance from a nearby chair to a battery of cameras. A small group of onlookers stood apart in front of the steps to the entrance hall. The solid wooden doors had been pinned back.

He narrowed his field, concentrating on the squat man in the centre of the group. Finally the set of head and shoulders convinced him. It was the same person he'd seen climb from the car into the blaze of arc lamps. He lowered himself carefully, dropping the last few feet to the ground. Gaunt's face looked peaked and tired.

'What the hell's going on?'

Hendry lit a cigarette, pulling the smoke as deep into his lungs as possible.

'They're setting up a newsreel interview. It's either that or television.'

Gaunt kicked uncertainly at the ground. Hendry held out the field-glasses.

'Do you want to go see for yourself?'

Gaunt shrugged. 'I'll take your word for it. They'll have to finish before dark. We might as well settle down here – it's going to be a long wait.'

Hendry grinned. This was the trump card your partner never expected.

'You're wrong. We couldn't have chosen a better time. There are fifty people the other side of that wall – all of them strangers. Everyone in the house is interested in the cameras – nothing else. You know something, you don't deserve this kind of luck.'

It was Gaunt's turn to take the field-glasses. He climbed

the tree laboriously. Back on the ground, he sounded anything but enthusiastic.

'I don't like it. Didn't you see there's a police car parked at the side of the house by the garage? It's asking for trouble.'

A guy like this could promote a tightly-planned scheme, backed by the resources of a government. He could listen to a hundred cops, wise about criminal expertise – but he'd never make a screwsman. To do that you had to believe that audacity made a sucker of organization. Hendry's voice was patient.

'You said we were going to do this my way. OK – forget all you ever learned about strategy and listen to me. Nobody burgles a house in daylight – right? That's why the windows are open. That means the alarm system's switched off. The cops are there to make sure some boozed-up electrician doesn't spit on the Bulgarian emblem, not for us. You tell me – who burgles a house with a carload of cops round the corner?'

He took Gaunt's arm, walking him back to the car. He unpacked the satchel, taking gloves, jemmy, and safe key. He looked up to meet Gaunt's speculation. 'I want to go, Bill. Don't stop me,' he said quietly. 'I'll bring your film back.'

Gaunt's face was worried. The effort to make a decision was obvious. 'All right. There's nothing I can do – you don't want me with you?'

Hendry was emphatic. 'You'd be a drag. I'll be out of there in half an hour. If it makes you any happier, go back up the tree. As soon as you see me coming, move the car to the gate.'

Gaunt picked up the field-glasses. They walked together as far as the wall. Gaunt looked up, almost as if he were going to scale it himself. Then he shrugged. 'Good luck. I'll be here when you get back.'

Hendry nodded. His outstretched fingers caught the top layer of bricks. He shinned himself, flattened and dropped easily to the other side.

The ground here was soft, the leaves sodden with last week's rain. The oaks stood in staggered lines, no more than three or four deep. In summer they would form a screen that hid the wall, creating an illusion of even more space. He had landed a hundred yards farther from the house than at his first visit. He was nearer the west rather than the east wing. A shifting sparkle of water marked the terraced pools where he had crouched. A no-man's-land of razored turf rolled between him and the bustle on the front lawn. There was no hope of leaving his immediate cover unobserved.

He worked his way along the wall, heading for the rear of the house. He ran, bending low, to a point in back of the garage. There the trees stopped. His progress was barred by a greenhouse. Giant chrysanthemums, yellow and bronze, nodded behind the glass frames. His cautious tread made little noise on the brick path. It led him to a courtyard. To the left was the garage. The doors were rolled up. A boxlike runabout stood dwarfed by the ponderous limousine. Both cars bore diplomatic plates. On the right of the courtyard were the kitchens and sculleries. A few doves pottered round a hose bubbling on the cobblestones. The voices from the front lawn, fifty yards away, were distinct. He walked casually towards the arch across the cobbles. The doves rose, whirring into their niche above the stable clock. Through the arch stood the empty police car. Its driver lolled with his broad back against the radiator. Hendry kept going. As he drew abreast, he was conscious of the man's cursory inspection. His own head never turned. Flower beds dotted the length of this part of the house. It seemed a long walk to the corner.

He moved briskly now, with the gait of a man who knows exactly where he goes. He was in the centre of the crowd on the grass. The rest of the police crew were deployed, slightly embarrassed and out of range of the cameras. The scene had the disordered bustle of a local fête. Cameramen were bawling at electricians. Maids leaned from the first floor windows of the west wing, their faces expectant. Hendry stood by a chair, unremarked and unchallenged. The small group of men in front of the steps broke away at a signal, reforming in the hall beyond. A table there was set with food and drink.

He strolled as far as the larger truck. He leaned against it, feeling the vibration of the dynamo on the other side of the panelling. A man wearing a beret leaned from the cab window. He spat over Hendry's shoulder with bored detachment. Hendry moved to the rear of the vehicle. From where he stood he could have heaved a rock through the open library windows. He wasted five minutes in indecision. The long, deserted vista of the east wing was tempting but it was still in view of the lawn. It had to be the front hall. The complete division of identities there must work in his favour. Ministerial staff and television personnel, each would accept him as belonging to the other.

As he started up the steps, the doorway filled with the people coming out. He stood to one side, allowing them to pass. The smile of the short dark man in the forefront was practised. He nodded briskly as the man at his shoulder pointed ahead. The large table in the hall was set with trays of caviare and raw ham, schnapps bottles surrounded by cracked ice. A manservant carrying a tray pushed his way through the baize pass door at the end of the hall. It was momentarily empty. Speed was essential. There was no certainty how long attention would be centred on the performance outside.

He slipped on his gloves and turned the handle. Noise mattered less now. He took the stairs, three at a time. The clock in the library ticked familiarly. A neat pile of letters rose in the middle of the desk on his right. He crept to the curtained window. The two chairs on the lawn were now occupied. The interviewer was leaning deferentially towards the minister. A man standing behind the cameras chopped down his arm.

Hendry wrenched at the bookcase, swinging out the hinged segment. The alarm switch was set at the OFF position. His brain seemed split in two. One part directed the key to be turned at lightning speed, impelling him from the house. The other provided caution, slowing the play of his muscles, parching his throat. Every remembered burglar's fantasy was suddenly vivid. Maybe the lock had been changed – the key had warped. Or once the safe was open, his fingers would close on nothing.

He felt along the bottom shelf, pulling the contents into the light. The top of the small aluminium canister was sealed with green tape. Rubber bands snapped it to a standard orange-coloured folder. He weighed the package in his hand. Something didn't jell. The sealed canister bore out Gaunt's warning of an undeveloped film. But the folder felt as if it contained en-prints. He thrust his arm back into the safe, groped along the other shelf. Only the stamps and seals met his touch. He pushed film and folder deep in an inside pocket and closed the safe. The view from the window was unchanged. The patient smile was still fixed on the minister's face. The interviewer's lips moved soundlessly.

Hendry ran down the staircase, stopping at the door to the hall. The unnamed sense that guides a thief's hand in the darkness signalled danger. He bent at the keyhole. The manservant's back was just visible. He was standing at the top of the steps, barring the exit as effectively as any alarm. Behind Hendry stretched the long corridor. A dozen yards along, the waxed parquet reflected a patch of light. A door there was open. He walked quietly towards it.

The elegant proportions of the room were unmarred by a partially-folded partition dividing it into two salons. On the far side, silver and glass shone on a table already laid for dinner. The furniture was baroque, every expanse between curves carved into heraldic emblems. Each surface bore the patina of age and ceaseless polishing. Chrysanthemums, their heads like those of unkempt poodles, massed in an old wooden cradle. The french windows were open, the lawn twenty feet away. He started across a carpet faded to new beauty. The great oblong mirrors set in white reflected him to infinity. He was halfway to the doors when someone spoke.

He swung round, locating the sound. The highbacked chair had hidden the woman from view. She was middle-aged with greying hair looped on top of her head. She was near enough to see the fine soft texture of her cheeks, the brilliance of her cobalt eyes. She was sitting facing the garden, a camera on the floor by her feet. The tilt of her head, the posture of her body, indicated surprise rather than alarm. She repeated her question, this time in German.

'What is it you are looking for?'

The distance to the trucks was suddenly increased. In his mind he heard the woman's scream repeated, the drumming footsteps as twenty people took up the chase. His hands in the gloves he still wore felt like footballs.

He answered in German, amazed at the calmness of his voice. 'Please excuse me. We're running to a deadline. I am supposed to call back my office. I was looking for a phone – too ambitiously.' He did his best with a look of innocent awkwardness.

Grey silk rustled as she moved. Her eyes were faintly worried. 'But Mr Davidoff is taking care of that. Were you not told that there is a telephone for your use in the hall?'

Flat planes ground the sensitive walls of his stomach. His inside pocket bulged with the film and the folder. He had the impression she was looking directly at it. He anchored on the name she had used.

'Mr Davidoff? No, they told me nothing. But I've been in the sound truck. I'm very sorry – you'll have to excuse this intrusion.'

She smiled, years younger and forgiving. 'There is no harm.' She pointed at the camera on the floor. 'I expect you have seen my husband – how nervous he is. He believes photographers to be worse than dentists. It is a lucky occasion for me. I have snapped him slyly.'

The artlessness of her words was too much. He found himself gauging her sincerity. He mumbled a reply. 'Many people find it an ordeal. I repeat, my apologies.' He turned resolutely towards the garden.

She was still smiling. 'But your telephone call. You may make it from here.' She indicated the sidetable by the fireplace.

He crossed to her side. Taking the instrument, he dialled

a number at random. As soon as the voice answered, he spoke with what he hoped was conviction.

'Wolf? Freddie. We're running a little behind schedule. I'll call you again as soon as we're ready to leave.' He put the phone down. 'Thank you very much. I'd better be on my way.'

She was on her feet. Before he understood what she was doing, she moved with the litheness of a girl and closed the french windows firmly.

'Nonsense. I do not believe you will be missed. There is time for you to drink some tea.'

She touched a bell-push on the wall. Resuming her seat, she smoothed her dress over her knees. The manservant from the hall answered her summons. Hendry sat nervously, the edge of his chair a springboard ready for use. He listened to the simple instruction, the brief reply, sifting the words for a hidden direction. The man bowed and retreated into the corridor. There was still time to make a dash for the servants' quarters – the courtyard and the shelter of the trees beyond. But even if he managed to scale the wall, a phone call would block every road junction in the area.

The woman's voice was warm and persuasive as if to put him at ease.

'I have never smoked but I quite enjoy the smell. What is your name?'

He lifted his head. She was holding out the oblong cigarette box like a peace offering that he accepted. He struck a match, committing himself to her sincerity. Instinct told him that the alternative would be wrong.

'Mueller – Freddie Mueller.'

She had a trick of nodding as she assimilated his answers – as if the sound of his voice were more important than his words.

'I won't ask you what you do, Herr Mueller. I am sure it is quite important.' Her gentleness precluded any sort of mockery. 'I am afraid we never see television. I have always thought that for the people who work in it there must be a sense of frustration.'

He pursued the thought uncertainly. 'I don't know. I

suppose it's like any other job, madame. Some of us like it – others don't.'

Her gesture included the people on the lawn outside. 'Look at it! Thousands of D marks – so much time and effort – to bring my nervous husband's face and voice into bars, bedrooms and drawing-rooms. Do you know what I like to imagine, Herr Mueller?'

He gave her the shake of the head she needed to continue. 'I like to think of a device that would register in the studio each time a set is switched off. A million hands pressing the button at the same time would be a corrective to pomposity. A man needs to laugh at the end of a day's work. I don't know – to drink beer, perhaps. But not to be reminded of politics. Do you feel like this, Herr Mueller, or do you believe in the importance of your art?'

He was unsure how he was supposed to think or indeed about what. The quandary was resolved by the arrival of the manservant with a trolley. The minister's wife poured tea into tall glasses with silver filigree bases. She floated a lemon slice on the brew, smiling. She was obviously poking mild fun at them both.

'The tea is Russian but the cakes are German. Rich and extremely bad for the figure.'

He forced the hot liquid down a reluctant throat. 'You are most kind but I'm not hungry.'

She followed his glance to the clock on the mantel. 'You must stay a little longer – at least till they are finished out there. It will please my husband. For him, talking to strangers is better than any banquet. There is little opportunity.'

He put the glass down firmly on the trolley. He was running out of time. He spoke courteously as he rose.

'I'm afraid I have to go, madame. The others are waiting for me. You wouldn't want to see me in trouble. You've been most kind.'

He unlatched the french windows and stepped outside. The cool air was a compress about his head. The desire to look back was irresistible. She was still in the same position in her chair. As their eyes met, she fluttered her fingers in farewell. He strode determinedly into the crowd. He was in time to catch the minister's closing words.

'. . . and through the joint efforts of our two great countries to achieve a permanent and lasting peace.'

Then the take was over. Someone bawled an instruction. The minister wiped his flushed face. He led the way up the front steps, relieved and animated as he talked to the producer. Maids bustled out, distributing refreshments among the crew. Hendry took a glass from a tray. The cops were back in their car. He could leave the way he had come only this time there would be a difference. The man who'd watched him emerge from the yard had been lulled by an obvious premise. The yard was an extension of the house – anyone leaving it had a right to be there. But the direction now would be wrong. Hendry would be a potential intruder. The game was too fast – too high and near its end – to employ the bravado of a boy-burglar.

The cold fire of schnapps chased the stickiness of the tea from his mouth. A hundred and twenty yards lay between him and safety. He carried his glass, strolling casually in the direction of the nearest lily-pond. It was sunk a couple of feet below the level of the trimmed grass. He jumped down and crouched, moving crabwise away from the house. A lifesize faun and nymph shielded him from the first pool to the second. He repeated the manœuvre four times. The few yards remaining were screened by a clump of rhododendrons. He glanced back at the men standing by the trucks. They were intent on the food and the drink. Not a head was turned. Their dismissal of him was as complete and indifferent as their acceptance.

He ran forward, the sound of the scuffling leaves reassuring. A hoist at the wall and he was over. Gaunt was nowhere in sight but the loose exhaust of the Opel clattered behind the trees. Hendry ran towards the noise. Gaunt was leaning on the open gate. The stretched skin from his jawline to cheekbone was the colour of cement.

Hendry tapped his breast pocket. The wish to crow a little was strong.

'I got it – no squawk – nothing.'

He bent down and scraped a hole in the soft earth with the jemmy. He stuffed everything he had used a foot underground. Gloves, key, and the jemmy itself. Then he raked pine needles, demolishing every trace of his work. He climbed up, dusting off his clothes.

'Have a look at the road. If it's clear I'll move out.' He angled himself behind the wheel of the station wagon.

Gaunt waved him on and shut the gate. The Englishman climbed in as the Opel turned on to the shoulder. He wiped away a moustache of sweat.

'I could see you go in – I thought you were never coming out.'

Hendry avoided mention of the woman. The episode was an admission of bad judgement. An acknowledgement that he'd carried the ball dangerously near his own line.

'You saw the production. The front of the house was alive. I had to wait for the right moment.'

Gaunt licked his lips, his voice almost prim. 'The film?'

Hendry reached inside his jacket. As he handed the package to Gaunt, the folder slipped from the rubber band. It fell, spreading the glossy prints like a bridge hand. Hendry bent down to retrieve them. The film must have been shot through a window. The folds of a curtain showed in the top of each picture. The man photographed wore dark glasses. He was standing on the edge of a jetty, looking at the sailing dinghies moored below. In spite of the foreshortened view and the glasses there was no doubt of the identity of the subject. It was Gaunt.

Hendry closed the folder, laid it on Gaunt's knee. He added the film. 'I took it on chance. They were together.'

Gaunt's thumb pressed into the soft metal canister. He cleared his throat. 'You did the right thing. We'd better get a move on.' His voice was perfectly normal but not his eyes. He was staring at Hendry as if seeing him for the first time. As though he had to remember what the Canadian looked like.

In that moment Hendry knew that Gaunt intended to kill

him. The world was suddenly vast and only he and the Englishman in it. He'd been as good as dead from the beginning. He turned away, a small thin voice directing him with cunning. It was essential to behave as though he had noticed nothing. He switched on the motor.

'I double-checked the box. There was nothing else there but these and the seals.'

Gaunt smiled. 'I seem to have saved my reputation for picking the right man. This is one burglary that won't be reported to the police but nevertheless the area isn't healthy. If they open that safe they'll be out in force.'

They drove through the hamlet and on to the *autobahn*. Night rose in the sky, casting lavender shadow across the fields. Gaunt's hands were quite still in his lap. Unnaturally still, thought Hendry. He'd have been happier if Gaunt had made his menace obvious.

Hendry set his nearside front wheel on the white dotted line ahead. 'The smallpox shot. You said they'd be ready for us any time. Why don't we drive there now. The sooner I'm out of the city, the better I'll like it.'

Gaunt's answer was equally offhand. 'No, I don't think that would be wise. We'd better go to the flat first. I'll be happy to hand over the responsibility of your money and passport. We can go from there to the RAMC depot.'

The words passed from one to the other, courteously deadly. The real meaning was hidden like cyanide in a sugar-coated pill. The voice in Hendry's brain grew louder with secret instruction. *The money and passport first, of course. That's when Gaunt means to kill you. Remember the gun in the bureau drawer – get to it first.*

'I'll call Bernadette from the apartment,' he announced easily. 'I guess you wouldn't want to meet her before we shove off?'

The smell of crushed peppermint was strong. 'No,' said Gaunt, 'I wouldn't want to meet her.'

They lapsed into an uneasy silence that lasted into the city. It was six o'clock. As the Opel came abreast of the corner theatre building, Gaunt came to life again. He nodded across the street. High over the pavement colour ran on rails, flashing briefly into a deserted parking lot.

'Run in there. We'll take a cab.'

Hendry's fingers tightened on the steering wheel. The front end of the station wagon bumped gently on to the ramp. At the rear of the lot he cut the motor and waited for Gaunt's next move. Anything the Englishman said or did now would be tailored to one end.

Fifty yards away, homebound office workers crowded round the trolley halt. The last shutters were going up on the stretch of cheap stores. A jukebox jumped in the bar next to the theatre. A woman with red hair was picking her teeth in the window. A neon sign overhead poured from an unending bottle into a never-filled glass. The street was lusty with noise and movement. Back here it was dark.

Gaunt eased himself out. They waited by the battered vehicle, timing the running lights above them. Blue flared then red. They broke for the deep shadow along the theatre wall, joined the bustle of the pavement. A half-dozen hacks were on the stand. Gaunt plucked Hendry's arm.

'Tell him the motel on the corner – that's near enough.' He climbed into the cab and wedged himself in the corner. The angle at which he was sitting kept his features out of the dim light from the dash.

Hendry relayed the order. He clutched the corded arm-loop, swaying with the cab's movements. The keypiece in the jigsaw still evaded him. He shuffled the bits endlessly. The solution came with sudden clarity. He had drawn the death sentence the moment he had bent to retrieve the prints from the floor of the car. The face on the film was that of a traitor not a hero. And only Gaunt had known it.

The cab skidded as the driver pulled across the trolley tracks. The two men in the back were thrown against one another. Hendry muttered an apology. He had an odd sense of anticlimax now that he knew the truth. He had no wish to destroy Gaunt – only to avoid being destroyed. He assembled his plan clinically. How he dealt with the Englishman depended on Gaunt himself. He probed, easy with the strength of his secret knowledge.

'What's my legal position in England now? Am I free, paroled, or what?'

'Free as a bird,' said Gaunt. 'Only don't go back there. You understood that at the beginning.'

The implication of a future was so well done that Hendry almost believed. Then he remembered the cold assessing stare.

He spoke without humour. 'That acre of beach is going to go sour on me yet. I can see it. I'll probably wind up digging bait for the tourists. Bernadette'll hit the bottle. We'll both get fat on bean fritters and blame one another for it.'

Gaunt made no reply. He was first out as the cab slowed, standing well away while Hendry paid the driver. They waited in the forecourt of the motel till the clatter of the diesel motor died. Through the shrubbery and into the school gardens, the Canadian was careful to stay to the right of the other. A sudden move by Gaunt would be easier dealt with from that side.

At the bottom of the steps to 118a Gaunt paused. He tipped his head back, looking up at the canvas-wrapped balcony. The top floor was in darkness. He opened the door. Hendry stayed close behind him, muscles tensed for the violence that had to come. The television programme was loud in the second-floor apartment, echoing down the stairwell. Gaunt used his key quickly and stepped into the small hall. The light switch clicked uselessly. Both men fumbled their way into the sitting-room. Suddenly the light blazed overhead. Hendry stood quite still, half blinded and not understanding. On a chair directly beneath the lamp sat Bernadette. Both she and Gaunt were watching the balcony door. It opened and a man stepped into the room. He dissolved the charade with a flourish of the automatic pistol he was holding. The silencer screwed to the barrel made positive identification. Hendry lifted both hands high in the air, the gesture instinctive.

Bernadette's eyes were still on the stranger. She came to her feet, closed the hall door and stood with her back to it, tall and pale faced. It looked almost as though she were trying to anticipate the man's wishes. Her obvious distress moved Hendry to anger. It was no trick to read trail here. For God knows what reason she'd come to the flat early – she could have walked in to find this guy waiting. Or he might have followed her in. From then on, she'd been used as a decoy. The plastic duck in the reeds with the guns waiting behind a blind. The muscles in Hendry's arms were aching already.

The blond man shifted his bulk, treading lightly for someone of his size. As he passed, he tapped Gaunt's shoulder with the barrel of the gun.

'On the floor, both of you. Flat on your stomachs and keep still.'

Gaunt was on his knees quickly. Hendry followed suit, lowering himself till the dusty smell of the carpet was in his nose. He felt the man's legs straddle him. Deft hands emptied his pockets. A shoe prodded him in the side. He rolled over on his back, looking up into the lights.

The blond man's tone was a parody of polite invitation. 'Now we'll have you on the sofa. One at a time. Come up very slowly. You first, Hendry.' He dropped the contents of their pockets on the bureau top. The pile was unimportant. Keys, a little money, the can of film and the prints. His finger tapped the breech of the automatic.

'At least one of you knows that this thing works. I'm desperate enough to use it. I want the bonds.'

Hendry was watching him cautiously. The words were incomprehensible but not the threat. The man's pale blue eyes were unwinking yet the edgy dramatics with the gun betrayed his nervousness. Hendry looked beyond the heavy shoulder to where Bernadette stood. Her face was strained – the leaping pulse on the side of her throat uneven in beat. She was intent on the stranger's every move, fascinated rather than afraid. He had to attract her attention somehow – warn her of a danger she didn't seem to recognize.

The blond man leaned far out from the hips, the top half of his body stiff as he considered Gaunt. He took three steps, bunched his left fist and drove it hard into the other man's belly.

'For luck,' he said touching the lump over his own ear. 'And if you don't find some answers quickly I'll do better.'

Hendry's voice cracked. 'Why don't you cut out the heavy stuff – nobody here knows what in hell you're talking about.'

Incredibly the answer came from the seat beside him. Gaunt had slumped under the force of the blow, his violet-rimmed eyes almost closed. But he still managed the boredom of the man who has seen the play too often – the voice of the fifth row centre that reveals the denouement.

'You're wrong, Hendry. Everyone knows what he's talking about except you. This is Mr Proctor. Mrs Jeffries loves Mr Proctor. They would both like to get their hands on the Benurian bonds.'

All that registered at first were the names. Benurian was easy. A memory of a trial – deserted smokeroom in a Frankfurt hotel. The fire he had fed with the useless securities. Last of all the swirling ash in the chimney, the end of what should have been the perfect coup. The name Proctor was more difficult. Then he had it. Gaunt had used this a couple of days ago. The full meaning of the gibe hit him. Only the look on Bernadette's face kept his fingers from Gaunt's throat.

She crossed the room, long-legged and smiling, to stand very near Proctor. Contempt gave her a savage handsomeness. She raised her chin defiantly.

'He's right, Kit. Two whole years and I'm glad.'

He looked at her in an agony of disbelief. He remembered the Sussex inn, the loose casements of their room banging in the gale off the Channel – the tumbled bed in the firelight. Her voice, low and sincere as she answered his question. *I'll never stop loving you, Kit. But that isn't a promise, it's an act of faith.*

He tried to swallow the burning lump in his gullet. She was lying. They were all lying.

'No,' he said loudly, and he knew he was talking to himself. 'No, you're wrong.'

Gaunt's recital was relentless. 'Mrs Jeffries is a determined woman. Her weekends with Mr Proctor weren't enough. She wanted the relationship on a more permanent basis. That's why she gave Detective-Inspector Pell the key to your cottage.'

Her dark implacable eyes made no secret of the truth. There was no need for her to speak. Hendry found himself looking at a stranger with familiar features. Suddenly it seemed the most natural thing in the world to despise her.

'You worthless bum,' he said quietly. In that moment he neither cared what came from the end of the barrel nor where it went. He wanted to tell them both that they deserved one another. He laughed openly at Proctor. 'You goddam fool — what makes you think you won't get the same treatment?'

Proctor's head swung from Hendry to the woman — a mongoose aware of a cobra. He turned abruptly, menacing the sofa with his gun-hand. His voice was pitched in shrill anger.

'How many times is it you've been inside — five? And you still haven't a pot to piss in. What sort of woman do you imagine you could hold? Get the briefcase, Bernadette.' His tongue whipped over his lips like a reformed drunk who sniffs liquor.

She came from the bedroom, hugging the bulging briefcase against her breast. 'Open it,' ordered Proctor. He dipped in, his pale eyes triumphant. He held up a package of money for the men on the sofa to see. 'Did you still think you were sitting on it?' His neck was dangerously red. He went into the back flap of the briefcase and produced three passports. He dealt off two, opening the third to study Gaunt's picture. He spilled the prints from the orange folder, comparing them with Gaunt's passport photograph.

He looked across at Hendry, his mouth puzzled. 'How does this joker fit in?'

The Canadian lifted his head slowly. The others didn't exist any more. He was going to jump this gun but first there was something he wanted Gaunt to know. The acre of beach in the sun — Gaunt's millennium — both were dreams. That's what he had to say.

'Tell him how you fit in, Bill,' he said softly.

Gaunt's feet shuffled. He turned his hands over and studied the palms. He said nothing. Hendry answered for him. 'He's an inspector of weights and measures.'

Proctor's lowered head swung belligerently. His eyes were suspicious. 'You bastards talk too much. Let's get down to business.'

Hendry gathered himself slowly. For years you wondered what made some men stronger than others. The answer was simple. They weren't afraid of dying. The first apathy of shock was gone. He was afraid all right but he still had to deal with Proctor.

'You're beating your tiny head against the wall,' he said ironically. 'There *are* no securities. Not here or in London. Nowhere. They went up a chimney five years ago.'

The woman caught Proctor's sleeve. 'I've got a feeling he's telling the truth, Philip. Let's get out of here.'

He shook her off impatiently. 'For Christ's sake, belt up and let me think.' He cocked his head, his eyes cunning. 'What about the money – did that come *down* the chimney?'

Gaunt wrapped both hands on his stomach, hunched as if he were still in pain from the blow. His head dropped gradually till the sandy hair touched the edge of the table. Suddenly he exploded into activity, jacknifing up with arms and shoulders under the solid wood of the table top. He drove it at Proctor like a battering ram. It cracked against the blond man's forearm. Proctor's mouth opened to show the fillings in his back teeth. He screamed once as the gun dropped from his useless hand. Then Gaunt had the weapon. He picked up the table, his breathing shallow and hurried.

'Make room for our friends.'

Everything had happened too quickly. It was a moment before Hendry realized that Gaunt's words were for him. He moved hurriedly, watching the man and woman take his place on the sofa. Proctor's face was the colour of a turnip. He was supporting his right arm with his other hand. Bernadette's forehead was luminous with sweat. She spoke almost humbly.

'Can't you see you've broken his arm – for God's sake let me do something for him.'

The gun hung loose in Gaunt's grip. His formal politeness only added to the sinister quality of the scene.

'How did you get in here, Mrs Jeffries?'

She pointed at Hendry. 'He gave me the key.'

Gaunt's head turned. 'Is that true?'

Hendry nodded. *She gave me the apple and I ate*. He had the hunch Gaunt wouldn't be interested in motive.

'Sure it's true. I sent it round by cab this morning.'

Gaunt's peaked features were impassive. He returned to the woman. 'Where is the key?'

Proctor groaned as she felt in his jacket. She held the key uncertainly then reached out to give it to Gaunt. He dropped it in his pocket. A bell shrilled in the kitchen. The suddenness of the alarm silenced the group in the sitting-room. Then Gaunt was in the hall, peering through the inspection glass in the front door. He tiptoed back into the room.

'The man from downstairs,' he said quietly to Hendry. 'Get rid of him.'

The Canadian shut the door behind him. He stood in the hall uncertainly. He could walk past this slant-eyed bowing kibitzer – out to the street and freedom. Without a penny in his pocket or a piece of paper with his name on it. And where did he run for protection – to the police? He had the feeling that for the moment he was safe. The couple in the room beyond was his insurance. Whatever Gaunt intended for him wouldn't be done before witnesses. The flat had become no place for an execution.

He filled the open doorway with his body, barring the little man's polite concern. He jerked his head at the empty socket in the hall ceiling.

'A bulb went. I was changing it and the chair broke. That's why I yelled. Thanks for inquiring.'

He waited till the bald bullet head had vanished round the bend in the stairs. He heard the singsong voice call and guessed that the Japanese was reassuring his wife. He shut the front door and went back to the sitting-room.

'He's gone,' he said flatly. The pair on the sofa were sitting close together. Bernadette's scarf made a sling for Proctor's arm. For some reason they both seemed relieved at his news.

Gaunt explained. 'We're losing our guests. Mrs Jeffries seems to have acquired an excellent grasp of the situation as it is. At any rate, for her sake, I hope so.'

She met Hendry's look, staring him full in the face. He bit on the last denunciation, aware that nothing he might say or do could ever reach her. Once they left the apartment, the duel with Gaunt would be on again. Only cunning could save him.

He shrugged, feigning indifference. 'What is this – a revival meeting? You've been saying it to me for days – she's a rat, isn't she? I'd put a hole in both their heads and worry afterwards.'

Gaunt squinted down his nose. 'I think my idea is the better one. Leave them to time and each other.' He came behind the sofa and leaned over, speaking into the woman's ear.

'Midnight, Mrs Jeffries. If you're not both out of the city by then, I'll let Kit handle you.'

She accepted defeat for Proctor as well as for herself. 'We'll go. As soon as I've had a doctor look at his arm we'll go.'

'For once you show sense.' Gaunt straightened his back and led the way into the hall. He unlatched the door and stood at the head of the staircase listening. He waved the pair out. 'Midnight,' he repeated. Their footsteps clattered below then the street door slammed. Gaunt opened the windows leading to the front balcony. He watched the couple across the school gardens and stepped inside again. For fully a minute, both men considered one another. It was Gaunt who finally spoke.

'I don't suppose it helps to say I'm sorry. I'll say it, anyway.'

Hendry's mouth moved but he said nothing. The air still carried Bernadette's scent but he felt neither pity nor regret. Only the dull desire to see day follow night and to be able to shut his own door. Freedom was a reason not an excuse for living. He watched Gaunt collect the things from the top of the bureau. Keys, film, and the folder of prints. The English-man lifted the briefcase on to a chair. He sorted out Hendry's Canadian passport. His thin smile was disarming.

'You'll still want this. And stow that money away some-where. I need the briefcase.' The gun drooped now in his hand as if he had forgotten it. He stuffed it into his waist-band.

The worn covers of the passport were faded. Hendry opened them at random. The Arabic on the Moroccan visa was like writing read in a mirror. It conjured up a villa with tinkling clocks. Beyond the orange grove below was the hard-packed Atlantic sand where he'd galloped into the rising sun. His first and last venture into the high ethics of commerce. They'd sent him broke in two years but not without teaching him a lesson. The law protected the guilty as well as the innocent. He felt suddenly old and empty. The memory was someone else's, not his.

He started to pack the banded sheaves of money into his pockets. Gaunt was playing it safe. Time was going to estab-lish their joint return from Haus Odensbroich. Now there were witnesses who'd seen them together. Gaunt's next move was obvious. He was going to be paraded at the RAMC depot and marked present for vaccination. It would be remembered that at X hours, Gaunt had left him, paid-off and breathing. The bullet would come afterwards – possibly from a stranger. For all he knew, Gaunt could still whistle up the help he needed. News of a dead Canadian with a police record wasn't going to burn any telephone cables.

To his own ears, the note of casualness was false.

'How about the smallpox jab?'

Gaunt was squatting in front of the empty fireplace. He touched a match to the film. The celluloid spiral flared. He added one print after another to the flame till all was con-sumed. He rubbed his hands carefully through the white ash, reducing it to powder. He climbed up and dusted himself off with a handkerchief.

'I hadn't forgotten. We'll go as soon as you like.'

Hendry's hope had been strong ever since he'd seen Gaunt

put the film and folder back in his pocket. He'd told himself there'd be someone at the RAMC dêpot who'd listen. Now he was left with a melodramatic accusation – nothing more. No film – no prints – just the memory of a look.

Sweat dripped ice-cold against his rib cage. He had to try to reach an understanding with this man. One last time he had to try. He found himself shaking and his voice was loud.

'You're crazy, do you know that! Can't you understand that I don't care whose side you're on. Not one hopeless damn do I give if you all blast one another out of existence. All I care about is *me*, do you understand? Going on living!'

The outburst caught Gaunt off guard. He closed the door to the hall. He stared at Hendry for a long time before he answered. His voice quiet and questing.

'And what's going to stop you?'

'Do you think I'm crazy?' asked Hendry. 'You're going to put a hole in my head.'

'And the reason?' persisted Gaunt.

Hendry accepted the fat, oval cigarette mechanically. Gaunt had a trick of freezing the action with a tag. *A reason for killing*. And what did you answer – were you real cute with something about intuition or did you just say that your guts turned to water because of a look?

He tried to read the solution in the colourless eyes but discerned only patience.

'Don't give me words, Bill.' He blew out the smoke without tasting it. 'I know my life's at stake – I can't win. But not yours. You're the one with the gun. Would you let me walk out of here now – the way I am – the way the others went?'

Gaunt's black trousers flapped round his legs as he rose. The nail rake had dried, angry on his stretched cheek. He pulled the automatic from his waistband and ejected the clip of cartridges. He brought as much drama to the movement as a man shelling peas. He tossed the clip at the sofa. It rolled on the cushions, finishing inches under Hendry's right hand.

'I've asked too much of you,' Gaunt said simply. 'That's a statement of fact not an apology. You've had a rough passage – now you can shove off. Any doctor'll fix you up. And good luck.'

The nickle casing of the uppermost shell was bright and polished. Hendry made no move to touch the clip. You schemed, bluffed or pleaded for what you wanted, to find it had always been yours. His relief was tinged with shame. The door from the apartment might have been a thousand miles away.

His face quizzical, Gaunt picked up the clip again. He carried it to the rear balcony. Shucking each shell from the container, he threw them far into the night. Then he fed the empty clip into the gun and placed it carefully on the table.

'Don't leave this behind. Leave nothing behind. Everything we brought into the place goes with us. I'm going to get the Opel again. We'll be with the quacks in a half-hour. Get the bags ready. See the lights are off and the door's properly shut before you leave. As soon as I'm back I'll sound the horn.'

The two suitcases were in the bedroom. Hendry carried them into the hall. Every bolt and catch was secured with the care of a nervous spinster. He stuffed the bundles of money into his own suitcase. It was a while before he could bring himself to open Gaunt's bag. He pushed his hand deep into the tumbled clothing. Through the thicknesses of material he felt a squat, heavy shape. It was the size and weight of a box of shells. He dragged it from its covering.

The leather binding on the book was mottled with age. The volume fell open at the first dog-eared page. Someone had underlined the passage with strokes of a broad-nibbed pen.

The moving finger writes and having writ moves on . . .

He replaced book and clothing and fastened Gaunt's bag. The memory that Proctor had already searched Gaunt only added to Hendry's feeling of guilt. He opened the door to the landing and sat down to wait for the horn's signal.

It came within minutes. He took the bags down to the street. Gaunt leaned across, unlocking the door of the station

160

wagon. He pushed the passenger seat forward, looking up at the darkened apartment. Gaunt laid the suitcases flat on the floor. He pushed the automatic along the seat.

'I meant it. I don't like these things even when they're empty.'

Gaunt buried the weapon in the glove compartment. The rain had returned, laying a wet film on everything within sight. Hendry slid down on his shoulder-blades, his hat tipped over his forehead. The windshield wipers clicked like metronomes, clearing arcs in the driving moisture.

'What makes your pictures so important?' he asked suddenly.

'You're mistaken,' Gaunt said evenly. 'There *were* no pictures.'

The rebuff was positive and unexpected. A belt in the rear for a guy who didn't know when he was well off, thought Hendry. He shrugged himself up in his seat.

'I was forgetting. You're right. No pictures – no safe – nothing.'

A sign flashed high overhead, a warning to reduce speed. Traffic signal lights showed ahead. Gaunt was driving badly, his foot hovering over the clutch pedal. He shifted the car out of gear, jamming on his brakes. The Opel skidded to a halt, the offside front wheel jarring against the kerb.

'Take it easy,' said Hendry, 'or don't you want that medal?'

Gaunt was watching the red disk. It changed colour and he let in the clutch again.

'If you're nervous, walk. It's the tyres – there's no tread on the front.'

The RAMC depot was in a solid stone villa on the road to Lohausen. A short gravelled driveway connected it with the highway. An oil-skinned sentry stepped into the headlights, holding up his hand. He came towards them, dripping rain. Gaunt wound down his window.

'Where can I find Captain Loder – I'm expected.'

The sentry used the telephone in his box. He returned to the car, touching the peak of his cap.

'The end door, sir. The white-painted one. Leave the car outside if you like.'

The gravel was raked and weedless, bordered by white-washed stones. The noise of men's laughter came from behind blinds on the first floor. They went into a hall hazardous with floor polish. A corporal was waiting for them, ears outsize under a regulation haircut. He looked bored and deprived of sun.

'Captain Loder's in the mess, sir. He says will you take a seat. He'll be down in a few minutes.'

They were in a room hung with test charts and posters about venereal diseases. An institution clock ticked over an empty firegrate. Gaunt flipped aimlessly at a bundle of buff forms on the desk. His mouth dragged with disapproval.

'Fall out the malingerers on the left! Christ, but this takes you back, doesn't it?'

Hendry sat in the middle of the bench. Gaunt was strangely nervous – touching and tapping with his fingers – his eyes never still.

'What's on your mind?' Hendry asked quietly. 'Maybe you guys really are unsung heroes but somebody'll pat your back.'

Gaunt's face was sober. 'I was just thinking. Millbank – the isolation hospital – now this. We seem to have got into a sort of medicated rut. What happens now – to you, I mean?'

Hendry gave it thought. Any planned hope had gone out the door with Bernadette. You went on, sure, but without direction. And that was enough.

'I don't know,' he answered slowly. 'A boat, maybe. If I keep moving – I think that's the answer.'

Gaunt nodded, his expression friendly. 'I'm driving to Aachen after all. That's fifty or sixty miles. You'd be a couple of hours from Antwerp – I could give you a lift. With that pair hanging around the airport I'd have thought it wise. But it's up to you. I'll drop you wherever you want.'

He stared back at Gaunt, seeing Bernadette's face through the crowd at the barrier. Beside her, Proctor. They were both smiling at him as if in welcome. No – Gaunt was right. Aachen was on the Belgian frontier. His mind leaped from the seaport to the shelter of anonymity. To the sounds and sights of the future, not the past.

'I'll take the lift,' he said with decision.

They both stood as the stocky officer pushed open the door. Black hair sprouted in the cleft between his eyes. He looked from one man to the other as though uncertain which to address.

'Good evening – I'm Captain Loder.'

Gaunt's manner was easy. 'I rang Brigadier Hubbold earlier today. Smallpox vaccinations.'

Loder showed a disciplined lack of curiosity. 'Ah yes. The Brigadier left word. I suppose you've both been done before?' He started to scrub up at the sink. His back was to them.

Gaunt's wink for Hendry was expressive. 'We've both lost count of the times. But anyway not within the last three years.'

Loder turned. His face was innocent. 'Take your coat off. Roll your left sleeve up as far as it will go.' He swabbed Gaunt's arm with alcohol and unlocked a case of instruments. He held the tiny scalpel like a pen, scratching gently till the skin broke. He touched the end of an ampoule to the abrasion.

'You fellows are lucky. We just got a batch of Canadian vaccine in. I find it produces the mildest reaction. Don't roll your sleeve down till that's dried.'

Hendry bared his arm while the manœuvre was repeated. Loder went back to the sink.

'It'll probably itch like hell – keep the scab dry and don't touch it with your nails.' He opened the book on the desk. 'Now comes the really important part of the operation. The book. If you've been in the army, you'll remember the bull. Name, rank and unit.' He scribbled the date and looked up grinning.

Gaunt's smile was responsive. 'Cripps and Hendry. Inspectors attached to the Board of Trade. I suppose you outrank us.'

Loder came out to the hall with them. He tapped the barometer speculatively. The needle dropped a couple of points. He rolled his eyes at the ceiling.

'Don't let anyone ever tell you about Manchester,' he said with feeling. 'It's my home town. But after two years here you even begin to *think* like a duck.'

The rain had intensified, falling in cold sheets, dislodging the gravel under their feet. Gaunt dragged the roadmap from the glove compartment. He held it under the light from the dash.

'That's it – the blue strip. Neuss – Grevenbroich – Jülich. We'll be in Aachen by ten.'

Hendry wasn't listening. The flap of the glove compartment was down. The gun was still there, lodged under the car papers. Somewhere at the back of his mind a memory formed and dissolved – like a weak signal on a television screen. Something to do with the gun but he didn't know what.

The impulse to get out was strong. When the car stopped at the sentry-box, he'd reach behind casually, take his bag and go. His arm was stretched along the top of the seat, his hand almost touching Gaunt's body. He felt his palm sticky against the upholstery.

Gaunt folded the map, orderly with its concertina creases. He flipped up the hinged cover of the glove compartment.

'Do you realize what they've done to you, Kit – prison and that woman? They've left you without one bloody buttress. Now you'll go on running without knowing where or why? You don't even care, isn't that right?'

He rolled the car to the sentry-box. Hendry rearranged his legs, watching with a sense of finality as the soldier held up the traffic for their exit. Then the headlights of the cars following replaced the man's figure in the driving mirror. The chance was gone and he'd done nothing about it. Now talk was better than chasing a fear without shape. Any sort of talk – even half-arsed stuff like this.

'I'm open to suggestions. Which would you recommend for me – God or glory?'

Gaunt worried the Opel round a bend. He was having trouble with the understeer. He slammed the car into an inside berth and braked to a stop.

'I think I'd better navigate – I'm giving myself the jitters.'

Hendry slid along the seat and took the wheel. The lighted streets made driving easier. He kept his speed down, cautious as he negotiated the streetcar tracks threading the south side of the city. Neuss loomed ahead, the racetrack vast and forlorn. The deserted stores were garish with night display. He stopped at the junction, looking across at the sodden queue stretched along the pavement in front of the movie theatre.

Gaunt's teeth ground on a peppermint pastille. He nodded at the welter of mackintoshes and umbrellas. His voice was sour and bitter – the words almost an accusation.

'Perhaps that's Western civilization's answer to your question, Hendry. Tits in glorious Technicolor. It's an easier form of escape than God or glory. And it has this virtue – you can get it for five bob and a soaking.'

The traffic signals changed. The line of giant trucks lumbered into motion, belching a poisonous cloud of oil vapour, iridescent in the headlights. They lurched forward, their drivers high in the cabs, bullying the smaller vehicles into a timid file.

Hendry pointed with a finger. 'They've still got their fog lamps switched on. I've got an idea the weather ahead's even worse than here.'

Gaunt's intensity had gone. He shrugged indifferently. 'Rain and fog don't mix. If it gets bad we can always turn back.'

Ten miles ahead, the first patches of fog started to drift across the highway. A yellow haze hung inches above the macadamed surface. Visibility was down to a few yards. The Opel shuddered along in second gear, fog wreathing the useless headlamps. Occasionally something crept by on the other side of the road – a vague shape lit by glow-worms. Hendry hunched over the wheel, speaking with his eyes intent on the road.

'I'm going to turn round as soon as we strike a clear patch. At this rate we'll be in Aachen tomorrow night.'

He sensed rather than saw the movement beside him. The angle of his head allowed a glimpse of Gaunt's lap. He was wearing a pair of gloves. For a fraction of a second, Hendry's foot lifted on the accelerator. Then the speedometer trembled back to fifteen miles an hour.

The picture in his mind flared into sudden brilliance. It showed an automatic dismantled to its component parts. The droning voice belonging to Happy, the small-arms instructor.

You can 'ave yer full clip, me perishing bleeders. But the bugger who keeps one in the breech dies comfy in 'is bed.

Gaunt had played his part with complete authority. Discarding the shells – leaving the gun with Hendry – gambling that the slug pumped into the breech would never be checked. He'd fed each cue with an actor's skill, setting the last scene on this lonely stretch of road. The fog and the rain were fortuitous. There were a hundred places between Dusseldorf and Aachen where a man could be shot and dumped without discovery.

He pressed his foot on the accelerator. He had to flush Gaunt into the open. His voice was flat and hurried.

'How long have you been a Commie, Bill?'

As Gaunt's hand snaked for the glove compartment, Hendry put the pedal flat to the floorboards. He swung the Opel off the highway aiming it at the verge. He pushed away from the steering column instinctively, grabbing at the hand that reached into the glove compartment. The car sliced through the hedge, teetered on the brow of the slope. It turned over lazily, rolling slowly at first then faster.

Hendry's arms were locked round Gaunt's body. The two men bounced from floor to roof and back, heads and shoulders thudding under the impact. The Opel slithered along on its back, wheels spinning in the air, then stopped. Hendry was smothered under Gaunt's chest. He kicked desperately, using elbows and knees. Suddenly he knew he was fighting dead weight. One last heave freed him. He held up a match in shaking fingers.

Gaunt's head lay at an impossible angle. The broken bolt of the driving mirror was driven deep into the skull above the temple. As Hendry watched, the body jerked twice convulsively and was still. The flame seared Hendry's thumb.

His first thought was to switch off the motor. The door on his side had buckled inwards. He shouldered his way through broken glass to fall on wet pasture. The lights on the car had failed. Here in the hollow, the fog hung, dripping and opaque. It invaded his ears and nose, blanketing sound and smell. He climbed up, wrenching open the back of the station wagon. He lugged his bag out and crawled forward, striking another match.

Gaunt's body was in the same position. A bloody froth seeped from the nose and mouth. Steeling himself, Hendry touched the bony wrist. There was no pulse. He groped his way to the inside pocket and pulled out Gaunt's passport. Feeling along the dashboard, he pressed the button releasing the glove compartment. He crawled out backwards, holding the gun. A hiss of escaping steam came suddenly from the broken radiator. He moved away, snapping the breech on the automatic. The shell casing was smooth under his fingertips.

He went down on his haunches, using the nose of the weapon like a turf-cutter. He slit a hole in the ground big enough to take both gun and passport. He stood up and trod the turf back in position. The weather would do the rest, destroying both signs of his footsteps and Gaunt's epitaph. When the fog lifted there'd be one more accident to add to its toll.

He picked up his bag and started the long walk up the incline. A mile along the shrouded highway he stepped into the path of crawling headlights. The car came to a complete halt. Hendry walked round to the side. The face behind the glass was startled but friendly. Hendry opened the door.

'Could I get a lift? I'm in the ditch back there – the steering's gone.'

The man slapped the seat beside him. 'Gladly. I'm heading

for Dusseldorf if that's any good to you. It's a bad night for walking.' He started the motor.

Hendry's knees cradled his bag. He was staring straight into the drifting vapour ahead. 'A bad night,' he agreed. But part of living was the hope that there'd be others better.

>>> If you've enjoyed this book and would like to discover more great vintage crime and thriller titles, as well as the most exciting crime and thriller authors writing today, visit: >>>

The Murder Room
Where Criminal Minds Meet

themurderroom.com